MIMIKA AVENUE II

A Novel By

Allysha Hamber

MIMIKA AVENUE II®

All Rights reserved © 2012 Allysha L. Hamber

No part of this book may be reproduced or transmitted in any form by any means, graphics, electronic, or mechanical, including photocopying, recording, taping, or by any information storage retrieval system, without the written permission of the publisher.

MIMIKA AVENUE II

Is a work of fiction. Any resemblances to real people, living or dead, actual events, establishments, organizations, or locales are intended to give the fiction a sense of reality and authenticity. Other names, characters, places and incidents are either products of the author's imagination or are used fictitiously. Those fictionalized events & incidents that involve real persons did not occur and/or may be set in the future.

Written by: Allysha Hamber

Edited by: Allysha Hamber

For information contact:

Allysha Hamber

Email: Lele4you@hotmail.com

Allysha4you@hotmail.com

Website: www.myspace.com/allyshahamber

Facebook.com/allyshahamber

Dedication

This book is dedicated to a very special person I lost right before completing this novel. Thomas Foster Jr. (Junie), my big cousin who was always there to support me in whatever I chose to do. He was an avid reader and a fan of my work and he always took the time to call me after completing each one. He knew every character by name, that's how I knew he enjoyed them. He always told me he was proud of me and that meant the world to me!

So R.I.P cousin... I know you're resting in Heaven, laying your head on God's peaceful bosom... I love you always!

To those who are so special to me. Never changing, never judgmental but always full of genuine love and encouragement.

Shouts Out...

Its 2012... Wow... I can't believe it's been eight years since I've dropped the first novel. I feel so very, very blessed! First and foremost, to my Heavenly Father for allowing me a chance to do it again... I Thank You with all my heart! My nieces ... Quionna, Miracle, Taderra & Meka. My nephews'... CJ, Chris & Cory and Lil' Ty. My two Great nephews... Tyree and Semaj. My God-niece... Shavona Bonner, Jayla and Marisha Johnson. My babies from another mother... Jordan Bonner, Justice Arties and Jada Bonner. My sisters... Sherri Jones, Maria Jones, LaNelle Jackson-Jones, Rhonda Jones. My Brothers... Christopher Jones, Wayne Jackson, Fabian Harris and Uncle Quinton. I love you all!

To my Peoples: Jean Whitby (Hey Sissy... Thanks for all your love and support.) Momma Whitby (Love ya!), Antoine Anderson, (Thank you for all your love and support.) Beverly Shelton, (Hold Me Down!) Cocamo (Always love), LJ (every since I met you at 104.1, we have been peoples and I love you for that!), L-B (My partner in crime... I'm ready to take on the world baby boy... let's get it!) Robin & LaDonna Foster (What can I say, you guy know I love you with all my heart!)

Guy Bonner: Nothing in life that comes easy is truly worth having! Difficult times make us stronger and God sees your struggles as well as mine. We have built a common denominator between the two of us... a family! I Love You!

FOREWORD

Hey Babies,

I know you all are excited as I am to be gripping another Allysha Hamber exclusive in your hands. So just imagine how I felt when I was asked to write the Forward. My palms began to sweat. My heart was racing as fast as a race horse and my brain was traveling like a speeding bullet flying through *Mimika Avenue*. .. Wow!

I had to control myself and slow it down; so what I did is I had a talk with myself. Now listen to the words I spoke to me. I said, "Mary just take your time and deliver to the readers what Allysha Hamber and her work it about. " Like the saying goes, the truth don't need no support, so with that said... here we go.

Living in the city of St. Louis, the State of Missouri, where the murder rate is above any and number one in the nation, one can only become an *Unlovable Bitch*. You try to carry this façade and *Keep It On The Down Low*, like no one has to know, but you know, *What's Done In The Dark* will eventually come to light!

So what's one to do in a situation as this? Well, for starters, you can try to get a decent education and attend the STL's number one high school, *Vashon High* and play hard ball or hang out with the *NorthSide Clit* which can only lead to one or two things... you can be judged by twelve or carried out by six, and neither is a good thing.

I asked that you all please permit this phenomenon author, Allysha Hamber to take you on a journey, which will leave you mesmerized and begging for more. All I'm asking is that you rock with her and she will roll with you. This will structure a relationship for life. I can witness that. So come on y'all, let's slide through the mean streets of the STL baby. Don't be astonished at what's in store for you. Just brace yourself and enjoy the ride. You're gone need to grip the ground baby, true talk. Mimika Avenue is nothing nice and this you will see.

Smooches, Dolls Faces and Don's.

Blessings,

Mary L. Wilson, Author of Ghetto Luv, Still Ghetto, No Matter What, Complicated and Tales of the Lou

MIMIKA AVENUE II   THE GAME HAS CHANGED

The saga continues...

As the weather has changed, minds have been re-arranged
but the concrete still holds prisoner cracks & crack heads even
more... deranged and doin' something strange 4 sum change
as the "odor" of the hood life walks thru any door and hangs.

This is still Mimika!! Ain't no warning shots tonight, just hatched
plots, continuous schemes & bogus teams whatnots... to many hands
been played, as loyalty takes a backseat, we treat each other as strangers
that live so close... we still feel like family but that's deep down
somewhere else as love plays no host!!

In between the quest 4 loot & the thirst 4 sex, grew the need to lie!
Even a veteran on the block was sure to make a mistake by not handling
thangs, or not try... a few made examples of those that were a threat to
his or hers hustle.
See the OG's that survived the 90's had done pulled a heist, but had lost
their focus thru half ass attempts & dreams that Mimika slice, that hood
pie ran the lint of empty pockets that's true life,
cuz a slice of the American pie, their dream, existed only in hand-me-
down loaded dice!

Rattling change, selling mouth, will keep any housewife pissed,
Puttin' in work and hangin' with killers like spider will only get an eager
chick's wet spot kissed intentions & shit not mentioned ran the night, the
spot, until pockets got swollen with knots.

Young bloods steppin up, & comedians always had Collard greens on
deck, yeah its funny... as legends tuck away they feelings only 4 peace,
to keep they game poppin',   ain't no trickin' though,
just hard dick, & bubblegum they coppin'... that's all they coppin' ... on
Mimika!!!!

Chapter One

Mystic sat in the back row of the Ronald Jones Funeral Home Chapel and reached down inside her purse for a tissue. The tears were falling from her eyes for so many reasons that day. It had been a little over a week since Spider had walked out of her life after finding out she'd slept with one of his business partners, Remo.

He was so furious with Mystic for sleeping with Remo, that he couldn't even begin to wrap his mind around the fact that she had only done it to get the bond money she needed to bring him home from jail. Mystic had somehow believed that he would adore her for going to any lengths to help her man but she was wrong. Spider couldn't see past the fact that she had spread her thighs and allowed another man to leave a mark on his territory.

Maybe if it had been a just a fling with an unknown niggah and he found out about it he could deal with it. Remo was someone he'd have to see on a regular basis in the dope game and that bothered him more than Mystic could ever realize. She had intended on telling him that night that she was carrying his seed but after he exploded the way he did, she figured it would be best to wait until things calmed down.

Spider hadn't so much as even driven down the block since that evening. Normally Spider made it his business to past her crib several times a day just so Mystic could get a glimpse of him lately; he'd been going to the store using the back routes. He couldn't stand the thought of seeing her. She had hurt him and Spider wasn't used to dealing with those kinds of emotions when it came to women, especially one outside his marriage.

His anger flowed through him so strongly towards her that he wanted so badly to hate her. Yet to hate her simply meant admitting to himself that he loved her just that deeply.

Mystic sighed as she reflected on how things had changed for everyone that night. The block hadn't been the same since all the madness had gone down. Everyone had lost good friends and the neighborhood was definitely different. It wasn't totally quiet but eerily silent. You knew something, better yet someone was missing, and now here they were sitting in the chapel saying their final "goodbyes" to one of the missing pieces to the puzzle they all called, *the hood*.

Mystic dabbed the liquid flowing from her eyes as she glanced over at her sister's Breeze and Punkin, along with Breeze's boyfriend, Man. Her eyes scanned the Chapel for Spider and she found him, across the aisle, sitting close to the front pew with his wife nestled beside him.

Mystic's heart was torn apart at the site of them with him leaning on her shoulder.

It should be me, she told to herself.

After all, it was her legs he had laid between when his best friend, Get Down had lost his life. It was Mystic, not his wife, who did whatever she had to do to get him home and it had been her who kept his secret of what happened the night Man's cousin was murdered.

How could he play me like this? How can he just turn his back on me?

Mystic understood that his ego was bruised but he had know that above all else that she'd proven to him and everyone else around them that she had his back, no matter the cost. Yet, she also understood that in a game like his, his status amongst his peers, especially the one he did business with, meant more to him than anything, including her.

Mystic shifted her eyes to the podium where one of the church members stood with the microphone in his hand and began to sing along with a voice so strong and powerful. He sounded as if the melody burrowed from deep within his soul and he sent a shock wave of emotion throughout the chapel.

"... This song's dedicated to my homey in that gangsta lean, why'd you have to go so soon? It seems like yesterday we hangin' around the hood. Now I'm gonna keep your memory alive like a homey should. A lifetime a memories, going down the drain, I'd like to keep stepping but I can't get past the pain..."

Mystic bowed her head and cried at overwhelming thoughts of everything surrounding her. Her situation with Spider, Get Down as well as the thought of never seeing Lil' Curtis again. He was always guaranteed to make her laugh or bring a smile to her face. She chuckled through the tears as she thought of him walking up the block in his pink bath robe, boxers and knee high tube socks. She would definitely miss him.

Her eyes drifted back to Spider who was clearly shaken by the words of the song. Mystic knew he wasn't just crying for Lil' Curtis but also for his friends, Kay Kay and Get Down whose funeral he couldn't attend because he was still locked up.

Mystic wanted so badly to run to him, push his wife to the side, grab him and just hold him close to her. In her heart she still believed that it was her that he wanted and needed, not his wife.

As the gatherer's stood and began circling the chapel to view the body one last time, Mystic knew she would finally get a chance to finally see him up close and personal as he passed her by. She watched impatiently as the ushers slowly guided people around the chapel pew by pew. Her heart began to flutter as his row came closer and closer towards her. Briefly they made eye contact and while Mystic's heart leaped with joy, Spider quickly looked off at the chapel wall ahead. He reached back, grabbed his wife's hand and pulled her closer to him. He knew this would bother Mystic and he was right. Knowing her eyes would follow him once he passed her; he quickly turned away from her and, hugged his wife.

Mystic's heart sank deep into her stomach. She felt nauseated. She had to get out of there before she threw up. She gathered her belonging's, cut through the oncoming line of people and rushed out the chapel.

She looked left and right for a sign pointing her to the restroom. She ran down the steps into the basement, found the restroom, flew into the stall, threw her belongings on the floor, leaned over the toilet and spilled her guts. She hurled into the toilet through tears of hurt and feeling of betrayal. She emptied her stomach of its contents, finally stood up, grabbed her things, walked over to the sink, placed her hands together and allowed the cold water to run between her fingers before splashing it onto her face. She couldn't understand why he was being so hateful towards her.

She looked at herself in the mirror and dabbed her face with the paper towel.

You got get it together girl. Punkin told you not to let him see you sweat and he'll come back. Come on Mystic, its big girl time.

As she exited the bathroom she was walking with her eyes to the floor when felt the strong grip of his hand, touch her shoulder. She looked up at him and all the big girl talk flew out the window just as quickly as it came as she felt herself being pulled into the comfort of his touch. She felt so emotional when she felt him wrap his arms around her that she laid her head upon his shoulder and began to let it all go.

He caressed her around her neck and rubbed his hand up and down her back. He whispered in her ear and softly assured her that everything would be okay.

"Blow that shit out baby, blow it out."

He pulled her face to his, wiped her eyes with his thumbs as his fingers softly slid across her cheeks. He gave her a gentle kiss on the rim of her nose.

"You aight? You know you better than this, right?" he whispered.

Mystic tried to look off at the floor but he held her face and forced her to look at him. She felt so defeated. She knew Man therefore she knew he wouldn't turn her lose until she gave him and direct answer.

"Yeah... thanks, Man."

Chapter Two

Tee-Tee sat on her bed and stared up at the ceiling. She had the radio on, a glass of cold Lipton Iced Tea beside her and thoughts of Cocamo running rampant through her mind.

She was wondering after all that had transpired between them, what his thoughts were concerning her. Tee-Tee wanted so badly to make things right with him but she had no clue how to go about it. Cocamo wasn't like the ordinary niggah's out on the streets. It had already taken so much for her to get inside his world in the first place. Once expelled from that world, she was clueless on how to get back through the iron gates around his heart.

She missed him so much. Missed the way he looked at her when she danced for him. She missed the way he would inhale his blunt, move to within centimeters from her face, pucker his lips up and blow chronic smoke from his lungs to hers. The way he talked to her when they had sex, so forceful yet inviting. He seemed so into her and she knew how hard that was for him which is all the more reason why she loved it. She even missed his sarcasm and his smart ass mouth because it made him who he was. Tee-Tee badly wanted his forgiveness not because she was afraid of what he might do to her physically but because she had fallen for him, she was in love.

Tee-Tee knew the laws of the game better than most of the niggah's in the hood and while she knew better than to think the conflict between them was over; she honestly didn't believe that he ever intended to hurt her. If he had, he would have done it. Cocamo was not the type of niggah to pull a gun and not use it. His hand was so tight around the back of her neck and Tee-Tee remembered standing there in the middle of the street not knowing which one she was supposed to fear the most, Big Slug or Cocamo.

To Big Slug hurting Tee-Tee would simply be business; for Cocamo it would be personal and everybody knows that personal beef is twice as violent as business beef.

The fact that she was still alive to tell about it gave her an inspiration that maybe in time things would be different between them because as personal as that moment had become in violence, Cocamo hadn't aimed his fury her way, not through the eyes of his .44 anyway. In Tee-Tee's mind, that gave her hope.

He felt something for me, I know he did. His feelings for me are real or I'd be lying next to that fat muthafucka in the morgue. I know he think he gotta play hard but damn, I miss him!

Yes, it went against everything the game stood for and for as long as she had been in the street life, Tee-Tee was all about the grind. She loved the money and the life style it provided. She had the heart of a hustler and she couldn't understand how Cocamo had broken down every wall she had built around her. Walls she had placed around her most delicate organ in order to survive inside the juvenile system.

Once the doors of her cell had closed and Tee-Tee knew she had to lay it down for four years, she set her mind to survival mode. Underneath she felt betrayed by those closest to her for allowing her to take a murder wrap instead of airing the family's dirty laundry. So inside those walls she would learn the grimy lessons of the real world. Lessons that made aware that she couldn't trust anyone but pay attention to everyone. Even the smallest peon on the food chain does what it has to in order to survive...

Tee-Tee took those lessons back to the streets and although she didn't allow too many people in her inner circle, she found herself the center of attention everywhere she went. Niggah's on the block respected the hustle in her. Even though she was pretty, it wasn't her looks that made them want to be a part of her world. It was the way she moved and protected her set.

Big Slug had watched Tee-Tee make and shake the scene for months before he approached her with the offer to join his camp. Tee-Tee was never one to take orders but she knew he could provide her with product when others couldn't make a way. Greed guided her decisions and almost cost her not only her life but the first man she'd ever loved and she wanted him back more than anything.

She picked up her cell phone, flipped it open and stared down at the lit up numbers as the radio played a melody that danced across her emotions.

"... As the sun sets and the night goes around, I can feel my emotions coming down. But now, as I go by, I cover up my face saying to myself tonight I'll forget. Tears, tears, falling down like the rain. Tears, tears, another heart know my pain... All the tears your heart wouldn't hide. Now the tears become a good cry..."

Tee-Tee let out a deep breath as she began to dial his number, slowly. As her fingers slid from digit to digit, she felt her stomach tied up in knots. She closed the phone and clutched it tightly in her hand. She couldn't do it. She couldn't face him hanging up on her or saying something that would crush her heart. Instead she re-opened the phone, went to her *inbox* and strolled down to his first message that she had locked into her phone.

"I don't wait on pussy, pussy waits on me; hand and foot ya dig... I'll holla."

She smiled.

How can a nigga that frustrates you so much make you want to be with him so damn much?

Tee-Tee loved the way Cocamo carried himself and his swag had captivated her against her will. As she looked down at the phone, she heard the pitter patter of her baby girl's feet at her door. Tee-Tee embraced her as she hopped on the bed beside her and guided her away from her wounded shoulder.

Her daughter was the best thing that had ever happened to her and in a way, Tee-Tee was thankful for the down time from the streets. After months of hearing her mother complain, it gave her some much needed time with her baby girl.

She lay there with her daughter's head upon her shoulder and realized that life was much to short not to go for what she wanted. If she wanted him back, she had to throw street logic out the way and listen to her heart. If it meant she'd had to bow down, she'd bow because to Tee-Tee it was worth it.

Tee-Tee flipped back open the phone, dialed the number and placed the phone up to her ears and waited. She gripped her daughter for support as her palms began to sweat. She almost closed the phone but she didn't. In her mind it was now or never.

Chapter Three

Man wiped a tear falling from Mystic's eye and let out a frustrated deep breath.

"I told you, didn't I? Didn't I tell you not to fuck with that nigga? I know how he operates. You outta his league. I tried to give you a few days to get yo' mind right after yawls little episode and this shit with Tee-Tee and Lil' Curtis but baby you gotta get past this.

You don't let no nigga, especially a married nigga, see you broke down and tripping like this. I get it. I get the fact that he was the first nigga you hooked up with fresh out the pen and shit. Being locked down for almost seven years is some hard shit, especially for someone like you. You ain't built for this shit.

The nigga shot game at you, you ate that shit up and fell right into it. I dig that but being locked down all that time ain't warped yo' brain and I know it didn't take away yo' fuckin' common sense! You ain't been gone that long to know the game ain't changed.

You don't bow down and cow town for a nigga who ain't fuckin' with you right now. Don't play yo'self Mystic, you better than that," he said, pulling her into his arms once again.

"I'm only on you because I give a fuck and I know you deserve better than what that niggah can offer you."

Mystic knew what Man was saying to her was right; she just didn't know how to take it in and accept it. She wanted to believe that Man was wrong and that Spider was just upset for the moment. That he'd come running back to her: back into her arms and stay there forever. She wanted to believe he would walk away from his wife and help her raise the child she was carrying.

Mystic believed with all her heart that Spider loved her, she'd felt it deep in her soul when he'd told her so and she didn't want to lose that.

"I hear you Man, but…"

"There you are," Breeze said, coming down the steps, interrupting Mystic mid sentence.

"I thought I saw you come down this way," she said looking at Man but addressing Mystic. "Hell, I came to see about you. I thought you fell in or something girl," she continued, wrapping her arms around Man's waist in a possessive fashion.

Man smirked to himself.

"What you crying for? That baby still kicking yo' ass?"

Man looked surprisingly down at Mystic's stomach as she placed her hand across her abdomen.

Pregnant? What the fuck? I know she ain't messed around and let herself get pregnant by that lame ass niggah?"

Man looked off at the gold speckled wall. He couldn't believe she could be so careless.

Mystic wiped her face.

"I'm cool, just a little overwhelmed at everything going on today, that's all."

Breeze looked at Man and then back to Mystic.

"Ump, well alright then. Come on, let's go. Everybody getting ready to pull out."

Breeze tugged at Man's arm and they proceeded to walk towards the steps. Man looked back at Mystic.

"You sure you good?"

Mystic waved them off.

"I'm sure. I'll be up in a sec."

Breeze snatched at his arm.

"Yeah nigga, she said she good, come on!"

Breeze couldn't stand the way Man always seemed to make such a fuss over Mystic. Breeze thought for him to be her man, he worried a little too much about what the happened to her baby sister. Mystic was a grown ass woman in Breeze's eyes and she had to live her own damn life, without Man always trying to interfere.

"I told you about always trying to be Captain-Save-A-Hoe to that girl. She ain't no damn baby, she can handle herself."

Maybe in her sister's eyes, she could but Man felt differently. He was the one who had gone to pick her up when the little niggah's tried to rob her when Perez put her out of his Cadillac after he had tried to get some oral sex from her in the park. No, she couldn't handle herself, not against the evils of the streets and Man was determined to watch over her, weather Breeze liked it or not.

He cared about Mystic, not because he wanted something from her but because she reminded him of his own sister.

Born three years older than him, Man's sister Mariah was beautiful, smart and had her mind set on being the CEO of her own design firm since she was little. Mariah was the Valedictorian of her class at Normandy High School. She was all set to go to Spellman the following fall.

The summer of 1993 had brought a lot of changes for Man's family, especially Mariah. It was the summer she met and fell head over heels for a big time drug dealer by the name of Black. Black turned Mariah out of a period of three months and Man watched helplessly as she went from beauty queen to crack fiend. Mariah, a shy and nerdy girl fell hard for Black a roughneck from the projects. He was starting to see a similar pattern with Spider and Mystic. No, he didn't think she would become a dope fiend but the attitude of doing anything to please your man or hold onto a man that's not worth holding on to, was eerily similar circumstances. Man knew that nothing good could come of this so called relationship.

It hurt his heart to watch her decline right in front of his face but the more he tried to save her, the further she got away. Black and his product had a hold on her, he couldn't begin to break. Mariah had overdosed a year later.

Mystic reminded Man of a lot Mariah's innocence and naivety before the streets had taken a hold of her. Mystic, like Mariah, fell for the excitement of thug life and unlike Mariah; Man didn't want to see Mystic lose the war.

He snickered as he turned back to Breeze.

"And I told you that color don't look good on you. You need to fall the fuck back," he told her.

"What color?"

Man chuckled.

"That envy green."

Breeze sucked her teeth and yanked away her arm.

"Whatever niggah, ain't no envy this way!"

"Shit, I can't tell! That's yo' muthafuckin' sister over there and you walk around this muthafucka like she one of these hoes on the street looking to steal yo' man. You act like you don't give a fuck about her or what the fuck happens to her."

"I give a fuck but she ain't gone listen to me. She do what the fuck she wanna do. She always have. I ain't tell her dumb ass to fuck with Spider. I ain't tell her dumb ass to go get knocked up. Hell when I did try to tell her something she went against the grain. Once I saw she was feeling that nigga I tried to slow her down and tell her not to get all involved.

I told her to use it for what it was but she did the opposite so now that's on her ass. I know one thing, what happens to her and who she fuckin' ain't none of your concern. I'm yo' concern! So you need to stop worrying about her so damn much and start worrying about this right here," she said, swinging her finger back and forth between them.

Man let out a laugh and shook his head.

"Oh ok, so you running shit now? I must've forgotten to check my messages for that bulletin. Since when do you tell me who or what the fuck my business entails? You better take a second and pull back that muthafuckin' attitude. You about to be like these muthafucka's out here that's three months behind on they electric bill… cut the fuck off! I run this shit, you run around in it, 'member that!"

He walked up the steps and headed back over to his friends standing by the chapel entrance.

Everyone was standing in line waiting to receive their orange *funeral* sticker to proceed on to the cemetery. As Man was greeted by one of the Funeral Directors he knew from the hood, he saw Spider outside in the cut leaning up against his truck. His wife was close but standing off to the side of him.

Ain't that some shit! Inside the nigga was all on her trying to piss off Mystic. Whack ass nigga!

Everything in him wanted to go outside and put his lame ass game on blast but two things stopped him. Number one he wasn't a hater. He couldn't be mad at Spider from a man's point of view for getting his issue on. If Mystic was down to be his PM chick then what could he really say? After all, he had PM women on a regular. Number two, no matter how fucked up as Breeze's attitude was when she said it, she was right. This thing between Mystic and Spider had to play itself out now that there was a child involved.

I wonder if that niggah know.

Mystic walked out the funeral home, stood on the steps and searched for her ride home. She found Punkin standing at the curb with Unc, who was on crutches to keep from putting too much weight on his leg with the injured butt cheek he received the night of Lil' Curtis' shooting.

Mystic walked over and stood amongst the crowd gathered only a few feet away from Spider and his wife. She felt so uneasy being that close to him but she had no choice but to hold herself together. She couldn't keep allowing him to see her constantly breaking down at the sight of him.

She was greeted with a hug from Toi.

"You okay?" Toi asked her.

"Yeah girl, I heard you were downstairs hurling and shit. You good?" Punkin interrupted.

"Ump, you might as well get used to that for a while," she continued, staring at Spider. "Morning sickness is a muthafucka."

Spider looked at Punkin strangely. He had heard what she said but the words didn't quite register in his head. He looked back and forth between the ground and Mystic.

Unc shook his head and chuckled.

"This niggah ain't got a clue. You ain't tell him yet?" he asked looking at Mystic.

Mystic shook her head, *no*.

"Don't you think you need to?" he asked her.

Mystic looked away across the street and whispered a solemn, "Yes."

Unc waved his hand in the air.

"It's all good, when you ready."

Spider tried his best not to look her way. He missed her something awful but he couldn't bring himself to let her know. She had betrayed him in the worst way and in his life style, loyalty meant everything.

Daily, he battled within himself to go over to her house and talk it out with her. He missed her touch, her kiss, her smell and they way she made him feel. He'd never doubted that she'd cared for him, she showed him that time and time again but he simply couldn't over look the fact that someone he knew, let alone she'd been with someone else on his watch.

A few nights Spider had parked outside their house in the wee hours of the morning and just stared at the house. The memories of the nights they'd spent together in the basement played in his mind like a beautiful melody until menacing thoughts invaded his mind, both unwanted and painfully. One night he'd sat there four hours confused about the way he felt. Now here she was standing within feet of him and still his heart couldn't decide which way it wanted to go with its feelings.

Spider looked over to Mystic, standing there wiping her face with a tissue. She looked a little ill to him but he looked away and forced his heart not to care. He turned and stared off across the street. He could smell the *Baby Phat* perfume he'd given her softly blowing in the wind.

Mystic had done something to him that not even his wife had been able to do. She had made him fall in love with her.

Yes, Spider loved his wife and family. That went without saying. His wife had provided him with a safe place for him to lay his head, keep his product and handle his business. Somewhere stable from all the kayos of the streets.

Yet, their relationship was nothing compared to the things he experienced with Mystic, not anymore. She made him feel alive again. Mystic had touched him in ways he never thought imaginable. The way they made love to one another was intimately new to him and he loved it. Which is why it enraged him so much that someone else had felt it too. Married or not, in Spider's eyes, Mystic belonged to him.

He balled up his fist and slammed it down on the hood of his truck forgetting that his wife stood within inches from him. He had to get away from there. Being that close to her made him want to do something to her and he didn't know if it would be a good way or a bad way. That scared him.

Everyone including Mystic jumped when his fist hit the fiber glass hood. She turned to find his wife trying to wrap her arms around him and him in turn, pushing her away. Everyone assumed that he was just having an emotional moment over the loss of his friends.

Mystic's heart broke for him and she wanted so badly to hold him. She knew that she was the only one who could make him feel better, just as she had done the night Get Down was killed. He had beaten her walls out of anguish and pain. Mystic loved every stroke.

She missed Spider so much. She watched as he snatched away his arm from his wife, walked around to the driver's side of his truck, got inside and slammed the door. He rested his head on the steering wheel for a minute and when he looked up, their eyes met.

He could clearly see the sadness in her eyes and she also saw the hurt and anger in his. So reminiscent of the last time they were face-to-face. This time though, he didn't turn away. He stared at her until his eyes began to moisten after she mouthed the words, "I miss you."

Spider looked down, exhaled a deep breath, shook his head and started his truck. He rolled down the passenger side window and told his wife to get in. He looked at Mystic one last time before throwing the truck into gear and pulling off. Punkin stepped off in front of her.

"Don't you say nothing else to him, you hear me? I know you see his bitch in the car. Don't be just blatantly disrespectful. Let his ass gone about his business. You said what you had to say. The niggah can play hard all he wants to but he'll be thinking about all this shit later on when wifey ain't around. BTSO (Blow that shit out) for now, aight?"

Mystic sighed and shook her head.

They all turned and began walking towards Man's truck. As they passed Cocamo's candy apple colored jeep, Mystic heard him call out to her.

"You wanna ride to the cemetery with me. Unc ain't going and I thought maybe you wanted to ride in a little peace. You look like you could use a break from the drama."

Mystic looked off to her sisters and back to Cocamo. Yes, she definitely needed a break from everyone, especially those who always had something to say about what she was going through. She was tired of Breeze and her insecure ways. She was tired of Punkin telling her what to do or not to do.

If she was going to get her man back it would take for her to do it her way, on her own terms.

Hell, Punkin can't keep a man and Breeze's man just uses her dumb ass. So what can they tell me about love? She asked herself as she climb into the jeep and put on her seat belt.

Cocamo looked at her and chuckled, "I bet you wish you would've stayed in the Aloha state, huh?"

Mystic chuckled.

"Sometimes but for the most part, it's cool. Pain in the ass or not, they still my family, ya know? Plus, I've met some pretty cool ass people here," she said, hitting him on the leg.

"Shit," he said, popping his collar. "It ain't a frostier muthafucka in Da Lou, baby!"

They both laughed.

Mystic liked that about Cocamo, he always made her laugh, even when she didn't want too. She knew his reputation. It didn't take long to hit her ears once she arrived back on the block but she didn't see that side of Cocamo. Yeah, he was super sexy to her so it was understandable that so many women threw themselves at him. He would often pick on her playfully and tease her about what he'd do to her if only she was his. Yet he'd never tried anything out of line with her and he'd always given her the utmost respect.

As the jeep pulled off and came to a halt at the stop sign down the block at E. Fair and West Florissant Avenue, Mystic looked over to her left. There to the side of her was Spider in his truck, looking like he was going at it with his wife. When he saw Mystic in Cocamo's truck Mystic could instantly see the expression change on his face. She could tell he was furious at the sight of the two of them together. He shook his head in disgust and sucked his teeth. As Cocamo pulled off, she read Spider's lips mouth the word, "*trick*" to her.

Mystic looked over to Cocamo and then back out the window. She felt a tear began to well up in her eyes.

Why is he being like this? It seems like he's constantly trying to hurt me.

Cocamo placed his hand on her thigh and squeezed it gently.

"These some bold muthafucka's out here, ain't they? It's all good though baby, fuck that niggah."

Mystic closed her eyes, tilted her head over onto the window, wishing that was exactly what she could do but instead she let out a silent cry.

Chapter Four

Spider sat in his truck fuming on the inside after seeing Mystic with Cocamo but because of his current company, he couldn't vocalize it. He knew Cocamo was a beast with the ladies and Spider always thought Mystic was so gullible to the kind of man. She had already proven with Remo how easily she could be taken advantage of.

He tapped on the steering wheel with his thumbs and grinded his teeth.

His wife was boiling on the inside as well for reasons of her own. She turned towards Spider and stared at him. It was time for her to get some answers. She had kept quiet long enough. She wasn't as stupid as Spider had thought she was. She knew who Mystic was. She didn't know her name or know her personally but she knew of her.

She remembered Mystic from being across the street from their house the day the police kicked in and locked up her husband. She watched as Mystic eased her way to the back of the squad car that was holding Spider and began talking to him.

Many times she'd sent her older children to the corner to see where their father was only to be told that he wasn't at Get Down house but down the street on the porch at some girl's house.

Spider's wife worked hard during the day at AT&T, trying to make sure her family was well taken care of. Yes, her husband was a drug dealer but unbeknownst to the hood, he wasn't a big as he portrayed himself to be. He could afford to flash his cash in front of the hood because she took care of the house and all its needs with her own money.

To her, the game could've brought enough wealth to help make a good life for them and the kids but Spider had two habits that took away any chance their family getting rich from the game… drinking and tricking.

She sometimes had to go looking for him and she often found him, laid up in some sleazy motel with some tramp. If she wasn't clowning with him over that, it was bailing him out of jail for a DUI or some other bullshit.

Regardless of his indiscretions and the bullshit he put her through, Spider wasn't always like that. His wife had fallen in love with a younger Spider, so full of ambition with plans of someday owning his own construction business.

Then his father died and left him the small brick framed house on Emma. Moving to the hood from the county had changed him. Mimika and its patron's had quickly become addictive to him and turned him into the man she now sat looking at with a major attitude.

She was fed up. Fed up with the way he lived his life and the way it always made her look. Fed up with the drinking, the tricking, the game and his going back and forth to jail. That is why she had refused to bail him out the last time the police took him. Once she had saw Mystic across the street, talking to him, she knew that Mystic had to be his latest quest.

Her suspicions were confirmed when a late night tap at the door awakened her a few nights after Spider's arrest. She answered the door to find a drunken Prez, standing on her doorstep.

Spider's wife allowed him into the house. As he sat on the couch, telling her how she deserved a man better than Spider and how he had just given the girl around the corner Spider's money to bail him out, it all began to come together.

She took the opportunity to questioned Prez some more about the "girl around the corner," knowing full well how Prez operated. He would tell you anything you wanted to know if he thought it would end with you giving up some ass. As she stroked the bulge in his pants, she listened as he gave her details about Spider and Mystic's affair.

By the end of the night, she had all the information she needed and more. She'd given Prez a little present for his information along with the slight feeling of satisfaction that she was in some way getting back at Spider for his constant betrayal by giving one of his closest friend's the ocean between her thighs.

Now that she'd seen it with her own eyes, it was even clearer than before. Spider wasn't just fucking Mystic; he cared for her, very deeply. She knew her husband, better than anyone. So she knew he truly had feelings for this woman. She now knew that his relationship with Mystic was the reason he'd been so distant the last couple of months. No matter what he did in the streets he had always made sure he got his fair share of loving at home also. Lately however he'd leave the block he'd come straight home and go straight to bed without so much as even attempting to touch her.

After watching him that day, she knew the worst had happened. Her husband was not only physically but emotionally involved with someone else.

"So what's up with you and that bitch?"

Spider looked at his wife, already irritated and barked out, "What bitch?"

"Nigga don't play dumb with me. You think I'm that fuckin' stupid? You think I'm blind nigga? You think I didn't see all that bullshit that's been going on between you and that bitch all day?"

Not only was Spider not in the mood for arguing with her but at that moment, Mystic was taking up all his available mental space.

"You'll come at me this bullshit on the way to the cemetery to bury my muthafuckin' partner! What kinda shit is that?"

"Don't give me that bullshit nigga. I don't give a fuck about you burying nobody from around that fucking corner!"

Spider was becoming more agitated by the minute but he tried to diffuse the situation to keep from snapping.

"Look, we'll get into all this when we get to the crib. Respect the day!"

"Ain't that about a bitch? Respect the day? Did you fucking respect me standing next to you while you gawking at another bitch? So, you fucking that one too?"

She already knew the answer but she wanted to hear him say it. She wouldn't dare let him know how much she knew nor how she'd found out the affair. To admit her own infidelity would take away the leverage she had in their marriage. People around the neighborhood thought she was a fool for staying married to Spider because everyone knew of his extracurricular activities. He showed no shame in his game.

However, Spider was her husband and she had invested a lot of time and money into their family, including the payments on his seventy-five thousand dollar life insurance policy. She loved him, true but she also knew the streets were a death trap and she needed to be prepared in case they caught up with him one day. She would not allow another woman to benefit from all the bullshit she had endured.

"What the fuck you mean am I fucking her? There you go on that jealousy bullshit again!"

"Jealous? Niggah I ain't never jealous of no bitch. You think I ain't see you cutting yo' eyes at that hoe when we passed by her in the funeral. Then you banging all on the steering wheel cause she drove off with another nigga, so what the fuck?"

Spider chuckled. Right or wrong, it irritated him that she watched his every move so closely. Spider felt that as long as he took care of home, she shouldn't worry about what he did and didn't do out in the streets. In his mind, it was all a part of the game; a part she accepted when she agreed to front him the money to get his weed game rolling.

"You trippin'."

She snickered. She was truly amazed sometimes at how dumb he actually thought she was.

"Oh, I'm about to show you trippin' when we hit the hood nigga, trust."

Spider started the truck, cut on his blinker and pulled out to join the procession. He really wasn't tripping off his wife or her idle threats. He'd heard them all before. Once again, she could assume she knew what was going on but she had no proof or so he thought.

Chapter Five

Cocamo waved goodbye to Mystic as she walked up the porch and he walked up onto his. After the cemetery, he had taken her to "CW's" restaurant for some good shrimp and conversation.

As he sat there looking across the table at her, she looked so flushed to him.

"You aight? You look like you need to lay down or somethin'."

She shook her head.

"Yeah. Umm, I don't know if you heard but I found out a few days ago that I'm pregnant."

Cocamo shook his head.

"Yeah, I heard a little somethin' like that. You know don't nothing get past me in the 'hood. So, what you gone do about it?"

"What you mean what am I gonna do about it? I'm gone have my baby."

"Why would you do that? I mean, why would you wanna have a baby by a nigga that belong to somebody else?"

Mystic turned away. She wasn't in the mood for any more lectures.

"Can we just not talk about this?"

"You brought it up. Let me tell you something Mystic. I shoot from the hip, straight from the hip. I don't sugar coat shit cause the world ain't gone sugar coat it. Why would you put yo'self in a predicament like that? You know from the flip two things that ain't gone happen. He ain't gone leave wifey, they never do and he ain't gone be there for you or that baby like you hoping he will.

That man got a whole family 'round that corner baby; he can't just up and be with you. So please tell me why you would bring a child into that kind of situation. One you know you yourself ain't gone be happy with? You got too much going for yo 'self for that shit."

"I hear what you saying Coco and believe me; I've thought about all that but why should I let what he got going on around the corner dictate what I do with *my* baby?"

"See, that's what's wrong with ya'll black women right there. That ain't just *your* baby. Just because he ain't carrying it don't mean he has no say so in what happens with it. That's *his* baby also and your decision not only affects your life but his, the wife's and his kids. This ain't just about you. And yes, I know he wasn't worried about his family when he was laying up making it with you but baby girl, neither were you. When you found out about his situation, you could've bounced but you didn't. All I'm saying is, why make the situation more complicated than it already is?"

"Cause this is what I wanna do! I'll be fine, really. I got this."

"Aight got this. You know how many women say that?"

"Well you said it yourself, I'm not like other women," she said, taking a deep breath.

She didn't want to argue with Cocamo and she actually found it kind of sweet that he seemed so worried about her.

"Look at you, caring all about me and stuff."

She smiled and grabbed his hand, trying to lighten the mood. She understood that she wasn't the only one going through a rough time. Cocamo had lost a lot over the last few days also.

"No seriously Coco, I'll be fine, really I will. I can handle this."

He sighed.

"I know it's been a rough week for you, too. I'm sorry you've had to go through all that also. I know you lost a good friend and someone you cared about very much."

Cocamo chuckled.

"You got half of it right. I've been knowing that niggah Lil' Curtis crazy ass since I first hit the block."

He looked down at his beer and twirled the nape of the bottle in his hand.

"The other situation is what it is. I mean shit happens. I let my guard slip but it won't happen again."

Mystic looked at Cocamo and wondered why he always felt the need to be so hard. She knew he really cared for Tee-Tee. She had him acting in ways he had never acted before with any other chick. It reminded her of herself and Spider.

"Well, I just want you to know that I'm here for you if you ever need to talk."

"Stop it… who are you, *Dr. Phil's* twin sister now? You can't even handle yo' own shit. How you help somebody else deal with the madness?"

"Shut up, I can too," Mystic told him, playfully slapping him on the arm. She picked up a jumbo shrimp from her plate and opened her mouth to receive it.

Cocamo watched as her lips parted and she stuck out her tongue to greet the seafood delight. He chuckled to himself. Mystic was so pretty to him. He couldn't understand how she'd chosen Spider to hook up with, especially when she had a nigga of his statue living right next door.

Mystic began snapping her fingers to the song playing on the jukebox.

"That's my jam."

Cocamo was tickled at her animation as she mouthed the words to the tune. He enjoyed watching her. He reached over and extended his hand to her. He wasn't big on dancing but he thought they both could use a good time.

Mystic placed her hand to her chest playfully.

"Me?"

"You better choose quickly because I don't wait on *nothing* to long."

She shook her head and laughed. He was so damn arrogant but it was one of the reasons so many women wanted him so badly. Mystic placed her hand inside his. Cocamo led her to the tiny dance floor and playfully whisked her into his arms. He wrapped his arms around her and pulled her close to him. She felt good to him and he in turn felt good to her. Simultaneously, they closed their eyes and inhaled each other's body scent.

Cocamo gripped her waist tightly and Mystic felt the hair on the back of her neck stand up. She didn't know if it was the music, his aroma or the couple of sips of wine she'd had but his touch was making her extremely moist.

She felt a quiver shoot between her thighs. Mystic leaned back away from him and their eyes met. They had never been this close to each other before and the attraction was so thick you could cut it with a knife.

Cocamo allowed himself to imagine for a moment; imagine what it would feel like to be inside her. He had always felt that she settled for less than what he felt she was worth. Standing there in his arms, looking into his eyes, her soul was calling him and in sync, their bodies were responding.

Mystic felt the large vessel hanging down the left side of his leg begin to grow against her skin. It sent a twinge down her spine and caused her to take a rough, hard swallow.

Cocamo leaned in closer and Mystic could no longer fight was she was feeling. She leaned in as well and before either of them knew it; their lips had met for the first time. For Cocamo, it was as if his lips had touched silk. For Mystic, it was intense, so intense she thought her knees would buckle.

The music playing on the jukebox did little to help the situation.

"... You're not alone, no. And no one's gonna hurt your heart again and this I know. You can count on me, I'll be there as

your friend. For no one knows the pain that you've been through. He took the best from you. Girl I know, you gave him all you had. You tried, when he played around. You cried when he let you down. You gave him everything you had and he treated you oh so bad... If given a chance, I'd make it up to you. If given a chance, I'd give my all to you. I'd teach this world a lesson and I'd never let you fall..."

His lips were so demanding and when their tongues touched, Mystic thought she'd have an orgasm right there on the dance floor. His touch and his kiss had an effect on her she'd never felt before, not even with Spider.

Omg, Spider! What am I doing? Omg!

She put her hands into Cocamo's chest and snatched away from him.

"Coco, I'm... I'm sorry...I shouldn't have... I'm..."

He wiped the corner of his mouth.

"It's all good. Don't apologize to me cause you feelin' a niggah and shit," he said, smiling. "Seriously though, I guess we better blow this spot before we both get into some shit. More madness than we already dealing with."

The ride home from CW's was silent between the two of them. As hard as they both tried to fight it, their minds were both on locked in what had happened. Neither had regrets but both were a little confused. Mystic was in love with Spider and carrying his child while Cocamo still had his feelings for Tee-Tee to deal with. Yet neither could deny that the kiss their shared had done something to the both of them.

When they arrived back on the block, they both agreed that they didn't want things to get weird between them so they decided to try and pretend as if it never happened; to go on about their separate lives as best they could. As he waved to her going inside the house and she waved back, they both knew deep inside that they were only kidding themselves.

Cocamo sat down on the black leather couch in his living room, staring down at the flower he was twirling around in his hand from Lil' Curtis' bronze casket. He was now alone with his thoughts and he tried so hard to come to grips with the past week. He hadn't really slept a wink since that night. Every time he tried to close his eyes and rest, the images played over and over again in his mind. The gunshots still ringing loudly in his ears.

Although things seemed to have moved in super slow motion but in essence two people lay dead within seconds that night. When Big Slug let off his two shots, Cocamo had instinctively pulled the trigger on both of his guns. He had hit his intended target and one he hadn't really meant to strike.

Everyone watched as Unc fell down to the ground clutching his right butt cheek with a bullet burning inside his flesh.

"Awwwww, Neph damn! How the hell you gon' shoot *me* in *my* ass!"

Cocamo was kind of relieved to see his uncle fall, not because he'd wanted to hurt him but because Cocamo's gun was aimed right at Tee-Tee's head and had she not ducked down when Big Slug fired, Cocamo would've blown a hole the size of a half-dollar in the side of her skull.

Big Slug fell back against his truck, blood seeping from his body. The pretty silver colored truck speckled with red down the side. He grabbed his chest as he looked to Cocamo. He looked wide eyed down at the blood on his hands, back to the hole in his chest and up to Cocamo. He tried to raise his arm and fire his gun one last time but Cocamo stopped him with one more blast.

When he knew Big Slug was gone he looked down toward the ground at Tee-Tee, expecting her to stand up at any moment and continued to plead with him for her life. Then he noticed the blood flowing from underneath her body onto the grey concrete. She was shot also. When Big Slug fired, he had hit Tee-Tee in her shoulder and she'd hit the ground.

Cocamo bent down to her, grabbed her and lifted her into his arms. Tears were rolling down her face as she looked up at him.

"I'm... I'm so... I'm sorry, I'm sorry. Please don't let me die out here. I got a baby... please... Coco... I'm sorry," she sobbed.

Cocamo yelled out to the crowd to call for some help. Punkin told him that she had already called as she ran over to Unc who was leaning over the hood of a car with steam coming out his ass cheek from the hot lead.

Cocamo looked over to where his uncle was and yelled to him.

"Unc, you good? My bad man, you know I didn't try to do that shit."

"I'm good Nephew but a nigga feeling like he got a golf ball stuck in his ass. Don't worry about me though, handle yo' business."

Cocamo returned his attention to Tee-Tee. He leaned down to her ear and softly whispered to her that she would be alright. He had such mixed emotions seeing her lying there. This was the same chick that was sent to take his life yet she had also become the same chick that he had grown to care for very deeply. The same chick he had gone out of his way to bail out of jail. The same chick he had laid with only hours ago. His anger had an edge over his concern for her.

"I ain't gone let you die. But know this; know that we ain't good Tee. This shit could've went a whole different way and it could be me stretched out on this muthafuckin' pavement. This ain't the time to get into this shit but know that just because I didn't cancel you out tonight, don't think this shit over."

Tee-Tee looked up at him through terrified eyes and painful tears. She really was sorry she had let greed and her love for the grind come between what she knew was something special developing between her and Cocamo. She understood his anger towards her.

"I know," she said, before her eyes rolled back inside her head and she passed out.

Cocamo didn't want to leave her there alone but as he heard the ambulance approaching in the distance, he knew he needed to clean himself up and get rid of his heat. He gently laid her head down on the concrete, stood up, ran over to the side of his house made his way around back to the garage. He hid his pistols before watching the ambulances and the police swarmed the area. He didn't know exactly how he was supposed to feel or what he was supposed to do. As he watched them load her onto the stretcher he pondered his thoughts wondering if he was supposed to stay or go. He was worried about her truth be told but he was also upset with himself for even giving a fuck about her welfare.

The time they had spent together had gotten to him, though he'd never admit it to anyone after everything that had just gone down. Tee-Tee had made his emotions mortal in front of the hood and that he could not take. He had a status that people both respected and feared. Even though Big Slug was handled to protect that status, Tee-Tee had shown the hood his weakness... a way inside. So his pride wouldn't let him move... he let her go.

He hadn't spoken to her since that night. He hadn't called and checked on her nor did he go see her in the aftermath. He would inquire through the grapevine how she was doing. It wasn't that his heart wasn't telling him to go and see about her. He simply couldn't chance letting her back into his world, a world she had almost single handedly destroyed.

He stared down at the flower and couldn't help but feel responsible that Lil' Curtis had lost his life in a situation that had nothing to do with him. Cocamo also knew that Tee-Tee and Lil' Curtis was very close to each other and he knew that losing him had to have really hurt her.

Subconsciously he had searched for a glance of her among the mourners at the funeral but she hadn't come. He didn't know what he would have said or what he would have done if he had seen her there and he was a little relieved that he hadn't.

He laid the flower down on the coffee table and walked into the kitchen to fix himself a drink. His phone began to vibrate on the table in the living room but Cocamo was in no hurry to answer it.

He hadn't really been doing much business since all the drama had went down and he figured it was just another one of his customers bugging him for something to smoke.

He walked back into the living room, plopped down on the sofa, grabbed the remote, turned on the TV and then picked up his phone. Whoever had called from the unknown number had left him a message. He hit the *call* button on his phone to connect with his voicemail, sat the phone down to listen to his messages and proceeded to roll himself up a blunt.

As he emptied the tobacco from his *cigarillo* into the ashtray, the voice on the line startled him.

"Hey Cocamo, it's me, Tee-Tee. I know you probably don't want to hear from me but I just wanted to call and say again that I'm sorry for everything. Sitting here in this bed has given me a lot of time to think about what happened and why it happened. I'm hoping that you can one day you can forgive me for all this. I understand if you can't though... just wanted to say again that I'm sorry."

Cocamo picked up the phone and stared down at the receiver. As he listened to the automated voice recording he felt kind of emotional. Then he sighed and looked off to the ceiling.

Is this still some sort of game she playing. I ain't been to check on her or said nothing to her. She probably thinks I'm still contemplating wiping her ass out so she feeling like she wanna call and smooth things over. Yeah that's probably it. Bitch ain't sorry."

He didn't know if he believed nor agreed with the thoughts running through his mind. He just knew the thoughts kept his feelings safe. He shook his head as the operator continued with her instructions.

"...to replay, press four... to delete, press seven..."

Cocamo sat the phone down and looked over to the flower. He took a deep breath and took a swallow of his drink. He reached over to the *seven* button but he found his finger wandering over and pushing *four*, over and over again.

Chapter Six

Tee-Tee sat up on her old wooden queen sized bed and began flexing her arm as best she could. It was still so sore and her range of motion was still very limited.

As she cracked her neck, she exhaled a deep breath, gingerly grabbing her shoulder. She stared at herself in the mirror as her mind wondered off to thoughts of Lil' Curtis.

She felt the tears roll down her cheeks. He had always been such a good friend to her. She wiped her face as she laughed at the thought of the first time she had met Lil' Curtis.

Tee-Tee was fresh out from doing her juvenile time for the death of her father when their paths crossed. She was at the State Probation Office waiting to see her probation officer when in walks a young brother who commanded everyone's attention as soon as he entered the door.

His voice was high pitched like *Screech* on the TV show, *Saved by the Bell* but his voice wasn't the only thing about him that would make you stop mid-stride. His outfit was just as alluring.

As he walked to the receptionists desk to sign in, Tee-Tee laughed at the Sunkist orange colored gym shorts he was sporting with his white, knee high tube socks. His tight fitting Hawaiian shirt didn't do him any justice either; filled with every color except the ones in his shorts and socks. He was definitely a sight to see.

After he signed in to see is PO, he walked towards the waiting area where Tee-Tee was sitting, smoothing out the many wrinkles in his shirt along the way. His outer appearance definitely put you in the mind of "Jerome" form the hit TV series, *Martin*. He sat down next to her, began to strike up a very animated conversation.

"What's up baby? Check this out, I'm like a caramel colored niggah right and I definitely got nuts. How 'bout you lay that chocolate all over me and let's make a muthafuckin' Snicker's baby! We could be so muthafuckin' satisfying together," he said, stomping is feet like *Sexy Chocolate* on *Coming to America*.

Tee-Tee burst out laughing and continued to laugh until her stomach burned and when the sensation subsided, instantly their friendship began. They'd hit it off from the moment he had opened his mouth. When they found out that they were both from the same hood, things just kind of came together. They began hanging out with one another on the block and Tee-Tee told Lil' Curtis she was worth her weight I the game and that she was ready to make money. Lil' Curtis in turn put her in touch with some of the other major players in the hood.

Tee-Tee blossomed at the game and she always looked out for Lil Curtis for helping her get her foot in the door. Out of most of the niggah's in the hood, she knew Lil Curtis was real and she knew he'd always had her back. It was because of him that Cocamo had known she was locked up and he'd proven it once again the night he'd lost his life.

Lil Curtis wasn't a hard core gangster. He wasn't the type to bang in the middle of the street. He was eccentric and funny. He could clown his was out of any rough situation. He was trying to do just that to save her life when he lost his in exchange, Tee-Tee felt utterly responsible.

Had she handled her business with Big Slug or simply told Cocamo what was going on, Lil' Curtis would still be alive. Tee-Tee wiped her face and sighed. To her, his death wouldn't be in vain. She would grind twice as hard to help take care of the three children he'd left behind. She'd be there for his mother and his sister but more so than that, she'd get back the man who had stirred up so much controversy in her life. Above all else, Tee-Tee knew that Lil' Curtis wanted her to be happy.

She had betrayed Big Slug because she'd fallen for Cocamo and Tee-Tee wanted him now more than ever.

She rose up off the bed, walked over to her dresser, dug inside the drawers for an outfit, laid it out on the bed and jumped in the shower. As the hot water ran down her face, down between her breasts, Tee-Tee washed between her thighs and she reminisced over the time her and Cocamo had spent together.

The way he'd walked up behind her and dove into her like a wild savage as she stood at the sink and cleaned his dishes. The way his jimmy grew and stood at attention when he watched her grind and dance for him; the way he washed her body so aggressively when they showered together. The way he would grow inside of her and he would grip her ass as he would unload inside her. Cocamo had done things to her body that made her cum like no other man she'd dealt with. She missed him so much and she was determined to get him back.

After she showered, she dressed herself in a cute short peach sundress that showed off the curves he once longed for. She lotioned her smooth dark skin with a *Dolce & Gabanna*'s Light Blue fragrance which drove his smelling senses crazy.

With one good shoulder, she oiled her hair, fixed her face, grabbed her purse and headed out. Her mom had taken her daughter to the zoo so she had the time she needed to try and gain re-entrance back into his world. A world that had went against the grain to accept her.

Tee-Tee walked out her front door and was met by Toi who was walking by on her way to meet Hank on the block.

"Hey girl, you feeling better I see."

"Yeah, it's coming around. I'm good."

"You know everybody just got back from the funeral. How come you ain't go?" Toi asked her, curiously.

"You know I ain't wanna see my nigga like that, not laying there all stiff and shit. You know that nigga just like I do. When you ever seen that niggah quiet or sitting still?"

They both laughed.

"Okkkkk… you shol' right about that one girl. Everybody was looking for you though and asking me about you."

"Everybody?"

She was hoping Toi would tell her that Cocamo had asked about her but Toi informed her differently.

"His mom's and you know some of the folks from the block."

Tee-Tee looked across the street at the alley that would lead her across Era and onto Mimika Avenue. At that moment she began to have second thoughts about going to Cocamo's house.

She wanted to see him but she was so unsure how he would react to her showing up both unannounced and unwelcomed.

What if this nigga get to clowning and shit. My feelings is fucked up as it is, I don't need to give him another opportunity to diss me. And what if he pulls out his heat on me? This shit is all still so fresh. I don't want this niggah to fuck around and snap!

She stopped in her tracks and Toi asked her what was bothering her.

"Was Coco at the funeral?"

"Oh girl yeah," she replied, hitting Tee-Tee on the arm. "He just pulled back up to the house a lil' while ago. Him and Mystic was together," she said, trying to be messy.

"Mystic huh? Spider must have taken ole' girl to the funeral with him," Tee-Tee replied.

Toi shook her head and Tee-Tee let her words and its insinuation roll off her shoulders. The last thing she was worried about was Cocamo and another woman, especially Mystic. Her head was too far gone over Spider to even begin to see anyone else.

Tee-Tee continued on her journey. When she and Toi reached Mimika, Tee-Tee stood at the end of the alley, stared down the block and started to cry. When she saw the orange funeral stickers in the windows of various cars lined against the curbs, she finally lost it.

Down the way through her tears, she could see the family gathered together on the front porch of the small brick framed red house. At that moment, everything seemed to hit her. She would never see her good friend and partner in crime sitting on that porch again. She wasn't ready for that reality, let alone dealing with his family or Cocamo.

Just as Tee-Tee turned to walk back towards her house, Cocamo came out of his front door and jogged down his steps. She watched as he headed to his jeep, unlocked the door and jumped inside. As he turned to get inside, he glanced up the block and noticed Tee-Tee standing there.

It was as if they both stood frozen in time, staring each other down. Tee-Tee didn't know what to do. She wanted to turn and run away but she couldn't. Her legs felt like concrete block and wouldn't move.

Cocamo made the decision for her as he proceeded to close the door and start up the jeep. Tee-Tee turned away, left Toi standing there and began to run back down the alley towards her house. She wanted to get away from the humiliation building inside of her.

She picked up the pace once she was out of his sight and when she made it through the alley and back onto Era Street, she felt a little better. That was until she saw the red candy apple colored jeep turn the corner and pull over right in front of her.

She stood there a second, looking down at the ground, her stomach tied up in knots as Cocamo rolled down the passenger side window.

"I know yo' tough ass ain't running scared."

Tee-Tee didn't know how to respond to his statement. She wasn't at the top of her game anymore when it came to Cocamo and the feelings she was experiencing over their relationship. It all made it even more difficult for her to speak her mind, so she just stood there and said nothing.

Once again Cocamo felt his heart began to wrestle with his mind. He could see the pain in her eyes and he knew she was hurting over the loss of their friend. Yet his own pain lingered from the betrayal he felt towards her and that kept him from being too compassionate towards her.

Tee-Tee felt everything building up inside her and she felt herself about to explode so she let it out, all of it. Her voice rising to its highest pitch. She fidgeted with her hands as she shouted out her thought at him.

"I was on my way to try and talk to you. Say I'm sorry in person for all this bullshit but when I looked down the street and saw all those cars with the fuckin' stickers and then his people… and you, everything got fucked up that's all."

Her tears continued to fall.

"I'm sorry aight! I mean muthafucka's act like all this shit is breeze for me. My fuckin' friend is dead because of me… me! And I almost got us both killed! Yeah this shit is fuckin' with me! It's fuckin' with me because I care niggah!"

The words had left her lips before she realized it and it was too late to take it back, not that she wanted too. She had just bared her soul to and now the overwhelming feeling of vulnerability had swept over her. The moment was monumental for her because even ion anger she had never opened up herself to any man.

She stormed off around the back of his jeep and ran across the street.

Cocamo bit down on the inside of his jaw. He didn't want to admit it but he knew exactly how she felt. The entire situation was fucking with him as well and maybe that was what was keeping him from her. Like Tee-Tee, Cocamo had never loved another woman besides the women in his family. His pride and his ego wouldn't allow him too. The home wrecker that had stolen his father from them and torn apart his family had seen to that. Yet, also like Tee-Tee, feelings had forced their way inside his world.

He shook his head in disgust. It literally angered him to feel the feelings and emotions he felt when it came to her but it was apparent to him that the situation wasn't going to just go away. He figured he at least owed it to both her and his heart to put it all to bed, once and for all.

Cocamo put his jeep in *drive* and pulled off after her once again. He stopped ahead of her, threw the gear in *park* and jumped out. He walked up to her and stood directly in her face.

"Look, I know you going through some shit right now too aight? I feel you on that. I ain't totally a heartless muthafucka because if I was, we'd be burying yo' ass in a box beside that niggah, feel me? This shit is all so fuckin' bananas! Like some fuckin' reality show bullshit."

He exhaled a deep breath, hoping he wouldn't come to regret what he was about to say to her.

"Get in; we can maybe at least discuss the shit."

Tee-Tee couldn't believe her ears. Through the tears her heart soared with excitement and joy.

Talk about it? We can definitely do that.

Cocamo got back in his jeep and turned to find Tee-Tee still standing there looking at him.

"You might wanna hurry up before I change my mind."

Tee-Tee wiped her face, walked over to the passenger side of the jeep and climbed inside.

"I gotta go to the store," he said, throwing the jeep into gear and heading down Era towards West Florissant Avenue.

"What's up with yo' shoulder?" he asked her, nonchalantly.

Tee-Tee slowly rolled her shoulder forward.

"It's getting a lil' better by the day."

There were no other words said between them. As Cocamo turned right onto West Florissant, neither one of them knew where to start although the DJ seemed to be riding along beside them in the jeep.

"… *Operator, get my baby on the line 'cause jus the other night we had a horrible fight. I admit that I, I was out of control, but I still love my man with my body and soul. And the road gets rough; we say things we should not say. But I never meant to treat my baby that way. I apologize, oh believe me I do. I apologize, honest and true. Because I know I was wrong and so I sing you this song. And I'm tryna get through to make it up to you yeah…*"

Cocamo turned onto the F&G's Liquor Store lot and opened the door. He ran inside to buy him a pint of Patron and two Cigarillo's.

Tee-Tee sat back in the jeep; listening to the music and thinking of how different the neighborhood would be without her partner in crime. So many times they had walked to this very store laughing, joking and smoking. They had some great times together. She would miss him a great deal.

She watched Cocamo as he exited the store and got back inside the jeep. When they reached his house, they both seemed hesitant to step out the truck. Finally they exited and he and Tee-Tee walked up to the door, both unsure of what awaited them on the other side.

"Aww, now that's what I'm talking about. Black love at its finest," Punkin said, sitting on her porch, smoking a blunt with Unc.

Tee-Tee smiled and waved hello to his neighbors. Cocamo nodded his head to his uncle and smirked. He didn't find that comment amusing at all. Once inside the house, Tee-Tee instinctively made her way to the radio and turned on some music. It was just like old times to her.

Cocamo smiled inside but remained quiet. Truth be told, he missed her presence in the house. They still hadn't spoken to one another and neither one of them was sure how to break the ice. Tee-Tee was the one who felt the urgency of the opportunity so she decided to use their favorite past time to cut through the tension.

"Is it aight if I roll up?"

Cocamo went into the kitchen and got a glass, came back inside the front room, popped the top off his bottle, poured him a drink and sat down on the couch.

"Do what you do. It ain't been that long. You know how I get down."

Tee-Tee rolled her eyes and frowned at his attitude. She knew this wouldn't be easy for either of them but it didn't have to be this hard either. It also didn't mean she had to like the way he was acting.

As she rolled up the second blunt, Cocamo downed a shot of Patron, straight. He immediately began to feeling the effects. He reached over to the table and grabbed one of the blunts Tee-Tee had rolled up, lit it and inhaled it in between dropping more shots of liquor.

The combination began to loosen him up, maybe a little too much. His feelings slowly mounted until they became uncontrollable and his mind could've gone in either direction. Before he knew it, he had asked a question that had instantly changed the atmosphere and put them both on guard.

"So tell me this, what the fuck made you *think* yo' game was so tight that you could honestly try and murk me?"

Tee-Tee dropped the blunt and stood still staring at Cocamo sitting on the arm of the black leather couch. She made no sudden moves, she just stood there. She couldn't believe he had asked her that and she totally didn't know what to expect next.

"I mean, this muthafucka sent you on a suicide mission you had to know that. Did you really think you could catch me slipping like that? Granted, a nigga let his guard down and got a lil' careless but you had to know I would be all over you the moment *you* thought you was cocky enough to make it happen.."

The thought began to enrage him and it scared the hell out of Tee-Tee. She was vulnerable. She had left her .22 at the house to avoid this very thing. She didn't want him to start thinking crazy thoughts. She didn't know what to do. She started looking around his living room for things she could fend him off with, knowing she only had one good arm to make it happen.

Cocamo slammed the empty glass down on the coffee table and Tee-Tee jumped. Before she could answer his question, he continued to tear into her, more aggressively this time.

"So what did you owe this nigga? What the fuck, were you fuckin' him too? I'm curious to know what the fuck you was gone get outta this, huh; money? He said you could climb the ranks?"

He stood up, put the blunt in the ashtray and reached behind the pillow beside him on the couch where he always kept a nickel plated .44.

The more he talked, the madder he got until he brought the pistol from behind the pillow and aimed it her way.

"I let you in my world, *my* world! You know how many bitches would kill to be where you were? I let you lay all up and through here like you was Queen B, thinking that maybe, just maybe you might be different from all these other bitches out here! You weren't though … you… you scandalous just like 'em!"

Tee-Tee heard the spite in his voice and began to feel the tears well up in her eyes. She assumed that when he said they could talk it over that they were past this point but she should have known better. Nothing in the game came that easy. She knew enough to know that this had to happen, questions had to be answered and feelings, no matter how bad they were, had to be expressed.

Her eyes widened as Cocamo came closer to her, gun pointed at her chest and his eyes red with a furious blend of rage and liquor.

"You thought yo' swag was that gutta that you could try to erase mine? Do you really know who the fuck I am?"

"Coco, please... we suppose to be talking about all this, not trying to re-hash it and go through it all over again. I said I was sorry and I meant it."

Tee-Tee stood up off the couch and backed herself up against a nearby wall, almost tripping over the multi-colored rug along the way.

"You sorry huh? What you sorry for, huh? You sorry you let that muthafucka control you? Send you into a war you knew you couldn't win? You sorry you weren't woman enough to finish the job..."

"I didn't want to!" she shouted through her tears.

"Or you just sorry yo' ass got caught? Which one?"

"No, neither! I didn't want too!"

Tee-Tee sobbed and her breathing became uncontrollable as Cocamo now stood within inches of her face.

She stared into his eyes and she knew it was then or never. She couldn't let it end like this, not again. She tried to calm herself and when she gutted up the courage, she began to speak softly.

"None of the above. I'm sorry I hurt you because... because I just wanna... cause I love you."

Cocamo jerked backwards and looked at her like she was crazy. He inhaled a deep breath, taking in her words while her smell forced its way into his nostrils. The words caught him off guard, the smell turned him on. He remembered it well. As his thumb toyed with the safety lock on the weapon, he repeated in his mind over and over what she had just told him.

I love you. I love you.

The alcohol fueled his anger despite the emotions he felt building inside his heart towards her. He wanted to hurt her so bad for hurting him; for making him feel this way about her.

He raised the gun to her throat, leaned within millimeters from her face, used the tip of the gun to raise her chin to his, looked her in her eyes and snatched her around her waist with his other arm.

"I should blow yo' fuckin' head off."

Instead of pulling the trigger, he opened his mouth, gripped a fist full of her hair, snatched her head back and devoured her.

The force in his kiss felt electrifying to Tee-Tee and her knees became so weak. The threat of bodily harm mixed with passion was somehow an amazing rush.

His anger flowed through his lips and entered her tongue. He wanted to hurt her not only with his pistol but with his jimmy. Wanted to break her back and hear her scream out in agony.

Cocamo put his forearm across her chest and gripped her shoulder. Tee-Tee immediately winched at the pain. He used all his force to spin her around and slam her into the wall.

Her painful moans stimulated him more and he desired to hear her scream. He spoke no words to her. He just unzipped his pants and pulled his pulsating jimmy from his silk midnight blue boxers.

Tee-Tee knew what was about to happen but there was little she could do to stop it, not that she wanted too.

She had longed to feel him inside her again. She wanted this so badly.

"I'm sorry," she whispered. "I'm sorry."

"Shut the fuck up," he barked, placing his arm into her back. He pressed her against the wall as he took his knee, shoved it between her legs and pushed them apart.

"I'm about to fuck the shit out of you."

His words ignited a fire deep inside her.

"Damn! Please do! Please let me feel this….let me feel you!" she panted.

Cocamo ran his hand underneath her sundress up to her panties. Quickly he snatched them off to the side. With his gun still lock and loaded at her chin, he adjusted his waist and knees until his jimmy found its way to its destination.

He could feel the heat beaming from the volcano that erupted between her thighs. Her juices, flowing like hot lava down the tip of his jimmy. Her moans invited him to go deeper.

He tossed his pistol on the couch behind him and gripped her waist with both of his hands. Cocamo plunged inside her hard, rough and raw. In his mind he heard Tee-Tee's voice but he saw a different face. One of a woman whose lips he had kissed only hours before.

He grabbed another of handful of Tee-Tee's hair and pounded inside her with all his might causing Tee-Tee to spray him with orgasmic liquid, running like an over flooded embankment down her thighs.

His thoughts of Mystic consumed him. He thought back to the way his lips felt against hers. How it aroused him in ways he never thought possible. The thoughts heightened his sexuality and he let his thoughts be known.

"Do you know how long I been wanting to get this pussy? Do you know how many times I've imagined being inside of you? Make me want it again! Make me crave it!"

Harder he thrust and louder Tee-Tee moaned. His jimmy was as solid as a concrete boulder, thrusting inside her, breaking down every orgasmic wall brick by brick.

Cocamo felt the heat within himself building. He reached around her neck and grabbed her around her throat with his hand.

"Get this nut baby cause I'm all up in you raw. Should be my muthafuckin' baby in you. I'm about to nut all in this pussy!"

Tee-Tee was so engulfed in the way it felt to her and she smiled at the thought of having her man back or so she thought.

Cocamo felt the tingle shoot down his spine. He saw Mystic's, not Tee-Tee's face, enjoying every inch of him and it drove him crazy. In his mind, Mystic gripped the back of his neck, interlocking her fingers as tightly as she could and told him to go ahead and let it go.

Gimme all of you, don't hold nothing back. Fuck me! Fuck me, Coco!

He bit down on his bottom lip and exploded not only in his mind but in Tee-Tee's body as well. He was in a complete daze. The aftershock was incredible. His body jerked, his chest felt like it had exploded and his legs melted like butter. He'd let off a mental nut that had taken the physical one to a whole new level.

When he opened his eyes, reality stared him in the face and Tee-Tee was standing there in front of him, stroking his hand that was still around her throat.

He pulled his hand away and slid his jimmy from inside her. You would have thought a water balloon had burst inside her the way their blended juices gushed from inside her.

Cocamo stepped back dazed and dizzy. He sat back onto the arm of the couch. He looked down at his unprotected jimmy, then to Tee-Tee.

Oh shit, I'm trippin'! I know I didn't just hit that raw?

He was so upset for allowing the heat of the moment to overrule his common sense.

Tee-Tee walked over to him with joy in her heart and a smile on her face.

"Did you really mean what you said or was that just a *good pussy* moment?"

"What?" he asked, looking at her confusingly?

"You been missing me and that you been wanting to be with me again and something about a baby that should have been yours."

Cocamo almost burst out laughing in her face. *Hell no he didn't mean it.* He wasn't even there with her mentally. He was totally *somewhere* with *someone* else when he's said it. He couldn't believe she'd be dumb enough to ask him that question.

Cocamo wasn't a dog ass niggah and he didn't want to hurt her feelings. He didn't have the heart to tell her he wasn't talking about her, so he took a deep breath before he spoke.

"Look, Tee…"

He wouldn't get a chance to finish his sentence. Outside a loud commotion had caught his attention and he heard a familiar voice that sounded in distress.

Cocamo stood up, put his sticky jimmy back in his boxers, pulled up his pants, walked over to the couch, grabbed is pistol and headed for the door. He wiped the sweat from his brow with the bottom of his t-shirt and looked over at Tee-Tee.

"You know where the bathroom is, feel free to do yo' thang."

With that, he walked out the door and Tee-Tee smiled to herself. To her that was an equivalent to him saying, "Welcome back." She stared at the door as he exited. His words playing back in her ear.

Should've been my baby.

She was elated to be back in Cocamo's life. Only she had no idea that someone else was now battling her inside his mind for the space she once occupied.

Chapter Seven

Mystic sat out on the porch with Punkin, Unc, Breeze and Man while they fired up blunts simultaneously and shot the breeze with one another. They were discussing all the events that had gone down in the hood the last few weeks, especially Cocamo and Tee-Tee.

"I don't see how that nigga can fuck with that trick again," Man stated. "You down with a nigga that tried to take me out and I'm gone still fuck with you? Bitch I could never trust you again."

"I don't think nephew really fucking with her like that. I think he just gotta get some closure to the bullshit. Ya'll know how Neph is, running around here all gung-ho when it comes to these females, like he could never get caught up with one of them. This one got him though; he was feeling that one."

Mystic didn't know why but their conversation concerning Cocamo seriously irritated her. She knew that she and Cocamo could never even think about being together because of the situations they both had going on in their lives. She wanted her relationship with Spider more than anything and she knew that Cocamo had his own thing going with Tee-Tee. If there was any doubt, the fact that she knew she was over to his house at that moment told her so.

Still, the feel of his lips stayed on her mind. His kiss had set her soul on fire and she couldn't stop thinking about it.

"Please," Punkin snapped, waving her hand in Unc's face. "He probably in there fucking her ass right now. You know how ya'll do it. Ya'll see very situation as an opportunity to buss one. You mad, fuck it out! You sad, fuck while you cry it out! You glad; fuck while you clap it out! It don't matter what the issue is, niggah's always think that banging up in some broad can solve it."

Man exhaled his blunt smoke and laughed.

"And ya'll don't? Bitches be on some wild shit too. I don't know where ya'll get that *withhold the pussy* mentality. Talking 'bout, niggahs' always just wanna fuck but then if we don't try and get none, ya'll be on some other shit like, who is this niggah fuckin' cause he damn shoal' ain't trying to fuck me!" he said laughing.

"Ya'll will twist the game in a minute," he said, laughing.

Breeze sat back and took in what Man was saying. He had her pegged to a tee. They had just gone through it the night before. She had asked him to be back to at the house at a certain time. Man didn't know it but Breeze was feeling freaky and she had a special night in store for him equip with sexy lingerie, strawberries, wine and whipped cream. As she sat back on her bed, candles lit and the love making music playing softly on the radio, she watched the hours pass by on her watch. She was furious when he showed up four hours passed the requested time. His excuse as always, he was hustling.

Breeze knew she always came second to his money and for the most part she never tested that. Every now and then however, when she asked him to cut it short and she thought she meant enough to him for him to comply but obviously she was wrong.

Man, entered the room and saw the candles almost burned down to the wick, the whipped cream melted and Breeze asleep in her sexy outfit. He was deeply aroused at the thought of it and climbed in bed beside her. He didn't think she'd be too upset. To Man, Breeze knew how the game went, MOB (money over bitches) always! That's what attracted him to her. He didn't have to go through all the bullshit with Breeze that he would have to with other women. Breeze understood his grind and appreciated the plush things it added to her lifestyle. Yes she complained about things every now and then but for the most part, his hustle was never a problem.

However, that night was different and as he rubbed his hand up her thighs, Breeze quickly smacked it away.

"Don't come in here with that bullshit now. I ain't in the fuckin' mood no more."

Man ignored the attitude and continued to rub the places he knew would set her off and Breeze continued to respond in spite. Finally Man turned over and put his back to her.

"Fuck it! You the one missing out on this good dick."

Breeze rolled her eyes and yanked the navy blue blanket over to her side and covered up.

"Naw niggah, the good went bad hours ago!"

Now she sat back on the porch and blew out her chronic smoke. He always knew exactly which of her buttons to push.

When they had first hooked up, it was all about business. Man had known the Jones girls' most of his teenage life. When he, his sister and his mother had first moved on Park Lane, Man often hung out all around the neighborhood and he quickly became a permanent fixture on Mimika Avenue. He quickly hustled his way to a reputation in the hood, beginning with stealing cars and breaking in houses.

Once he got turned on to the dope game, he never looked back. Man put in the time and the work necessary to reach the top.

He'd just about done dirt with every real nigga in the hood and he'd gained the respect of all the major players in the game.

Man never set out to cheat anyone in the game because he understood that most of the niggah's that was deep in the game was just like him, meaning they would kill for theirs the same as he would.

When Man began to notice the three maturing girls growing up at 5954, he paid close attention to the way they moved. The eldest was a hefty girl with a very pretty face that Man saw as not only a loyal weed customer but a cool sistah he could sit back, talk shit and chill with, like one of his boys. They had become really good friends over the years.

The youngest was a cute but skinny little girl who was always running up behind the older crowd, trying to hang out. Man thought of her as a pain-in-the ass little sister and he often gave her pocket change to run back and forth to the store. Once she graduated from high school, she'd gotten married and left the hood. It had hurt Man to see her go through the things she had gone through. She had literally become a woman right before his eyes and he knew that that she wasn't built like the other two girls in her family. She was a different breed and he felt the need to watch over her from afar.

The middle sister though, thick and sassy one that always had something smart to say was the toughest of the crew and he loved the fight in her.

Man would watch her get out in the streets and bang with three girls at once and hold her own. He loved it and he knew she was the right type of girl to be at his side in the streets because she would definitely have his back.

She didn't disappoint him either; she stood her ground, she learned the game, she followed his lead, she did what she was told and she quickly became Queen B of his crew and his heart. Although Man would never say that they were officially a couple. She knew he would give her the world as long as she stayed in her lane but every now and then like the night before, Breeze longed for a normal relationship. One with a man she knew would always have the time for her when she needed to feel special.

"Whatever nigga, if ya'll act like ya'll had some damn sense we wouldn't have to clown ya'll," Breeze stated. "Pussy ain't like toilet tissue niggah; you can't just roll this shit off and use it when you want to!"

Mystic tuned out the conversation and turned over the writing pad where she often jotted down her thoughts and began writing on a fresh piece of paper.

She thought of Breeze and Man and the way they were together as her pen flowed against the paper. With her room right next door, whenever they were into it, she knew about it. Most of the time, it was because Man couldn't stay out the streets long enough to pay her some much needed attention.

"The Hood in You"

This is for all the times that I've complained, you're always in the streets.

Even though in my heart I know you're doing what you gotta do so me and our kids can eat.

Living your life by the code of the streets, "Get money by any means necessary."

And even though it comes off like I'm bitchin', it's just for your safety Boo, I worry.

For all the late nights I've accused you of creeping, you tell me to chill, you're on the grind.

It's just that I want you at home with me, in bed, our legs intertwined.

For the times I call and you don't answer and I'm at home going half crazy.

It's not that I'm trying to blow you up, it's just, I may really need you baby.

What I'm trying to say is, don't take me wrong, I respect both the grind and what you do.

And I'll always love and appreciate the man you are but most of all the 'hood in you.

"Look at this shit ya'll," Punkin said, taking Mystic away from her thoughts.

Everyone looked up from what they were doing to see Spider coming around the corner with a slight crowd following behind.

You could hear his wife's voice half way down the block yelling and cursing at him. He tried to cross the street onto Harvey where his boys DC and Tank was chilling at but his wife stood in the middle of the street, blocking his path.

"Oh, so you ain't gone do it?" They heard her ask him.

Spider pushed her off to the side and continued to turn up his bottle of MD 20/20. His wife in turn, jumped back in front of him and swatted the bottle out his hand, sending to it crashing onto the concrete below.

Across the way Harvey, DC and Tank came off the porch to be nosey, followed by Toi and Hank. Mystic stood up from off the ledge, watching intensely.

Why the hell does she always gotta clown him in public in front of everybody. That's why he cheat on her ass now, stupid bitch!

Punkin, Breeze and Man all came down the off the porch and walked down to the curb to get a better view of the drama.

"It's some bullshit about to go down; watch what I tell ya'll. This hoe about to show her ass out here," Punkin said.

"Yeah well, all I know is she better keep that shit up the way where it belong; aimed at her sorry ass man. Don't bring that noise down here to my muthafuckin' sister," Breeze chimed in.

This was the side of Breeze that Man loved to see and he was so damn turned on at that moment. He walked up behind her and smacked her on her ass.

"Now that's what I'm talking about. You know I'm fucking the shit out of you when this over."

Breeze laughed and pushed him away.

"Nigga you know I ain't about to let nobody fuck with my sisters. I'll beat that hoe's ass today! Don't bring that bullshit on the block cause you mad that you can't control *yo'* man!"

Man looked back at Mystic standing on the steps. She put down her notebook, trotted down the steps and joined her folks on the curb. She couldn't phantom the thought of this having anything to do with her.

Man smirked as he looked at her.

"Now you about to see what I'm talkin' about."

"Why you say that? This ain't got nothing to do with me, Man."

Punkin spun around and shook her head.

"How come it don't? Me or Breeze ain't creeping with her husband," she stated.

Punkin couldn't believe how oblivious to the world Mystic could be sometimes.

"What the hell you think it's about? You ever seen them out here like this? You ever seen that woman on the block before acting like this? That woman ain't stupid! She got eyes. You don't think she seen all that bullshit between ya'll at the funeral today? Oh, yes sweetie, this all about you! I told you, you wanna be a big girl and play big girl games? Well, it's time to face the consequences like a big girl."

By this time, Unc had also made it down to the curb. He was still moving slow from Cocamo's bullet in his ass.

Unc yelled out to Spider up the way and told him to take his business back around the corner.

"Don't have yo' wife out here acting like this man; giving folks a show and something to talk about. Go handle yo' shit and then come back to the block!"

Spider held his hands up in the air.

"Unc she wanna make a muthafuckin' spectacle of herself in front of everybody then I'm gone let her. Cause this bullshit she on, she on by herself."

"So you gone let her stand out here and put on a show and shit nigga?" Unc asked his voice elevating.

The rise in his tone of voice brought Cocamo out onto the porch to check on him. Once outside Cocamo saw the crowd that had gathered in front of the house and he looked off up the street at what they had gathered to see.

He walked down the steps and over to Unc.

"You good Unc?"

"Yeah Neph, I'm good. I'm just trying to tell this niggah to take this bullshit back around the corner and stop setting his damn business all out in front of everybody."

Breeze popped her fist inside her hand.

"I know that hoe better not bring that drama to my sister, that's all I know!"

Cocamo looked over to Mystic who wouldn't return his glare. She just looked at the ground. When he asked her if she was okay, she just hunched her shoulders.

"I don't think any of this has to do with me but they do," she said, swinging her arm around at the crowd.

Cocamo grabbed her arm and turned her towards him, still tripping off the previous thoughts he'd had of her just moments before.

She turned her body to him but she couldn't bring herself to face him. She didn't know why, she just couldn't. The business with Tee-Tee, right or wrong, bothered her more than she'd realized.

Cocamo pulled her away to the side, sensing something was wrong.

"What's on yo' mind with all this going on?"

"Like you care," she snapped back.

"Aye, that in there ain't what you thinking. I just was trying to get a grip on some of this shit that went down, that's all it is."

"You don't owe me no explanation Coco, we friends. I ain't trippin'. I mean that kiss didn't mean anything, right? You got her and me; well I'm having a baby by someone else."

He caught the sarcasm in her voice and it was clear to him that that kiss meant more to both of them than either one of them wanted to admit.

Before he could respond, Spider's wife started up again. This time she let every bystander know what was on her mind.

"You want me to believe you ain't fuckin' with that bitch, you gone take yo' ass down there and tell her to her face you ain't fuckin' with her. Let's go nigga!"

Punkin turned to Mystic with her hand on one hip and the other wrapped around her blunt.

"Yo' naive ass still think this ain't got nothing to do with you? I know what the hell I be talking about. I know how this shit work."

Mystic's stomach instantly turned into knots. What would she do if Spider came to her and spoke those hurtful words directly to her face? More so, she wondered what she'd have to do if his wife followed suit behind him. Mystic wasn't the type to start drama or be as vocal as her sisters but she was raised in the same house as them, meaning she would get down if she had too. The only thing that would stop her was the thought of hurting her unborn child. That she could not deal with.

Man lit his Newport and glanced over at Cocamo.

"You strapped?"

Cocamo looked to Mystic and then back to Man.

"Always," Cocamo answered him, patting the back of his waist.

Mystic was now getting worried. She couldn't believe all this was happening but Man knew how these situations could spin out of control. On the corner were Spider's two almost grown sons. They were young thunder cats that loved to get into mischief. If this boiled over they would be ready to protect their mother at any cost. Man both respected and understood that but it didn't mean that he would let that shit go down. If any resident of 5954 had static, so did he. He loved them all like that.

"Take yo' ass down there! What you scared? That bitch got some kinda hold on you or somethin'? You won't go? I'll go," she screamed, turning to come down the block.

"If that nigga come down here with that lame shit, I'm whooping his ass and this shit gone get real ugly," Man stated, matter-of-factly.

"I hear that," Cocamo joined in. "I ain't got shit against that niggah but if he get on this hoe shit, he need his ass whooped!"

Punkin continued to inhale the smoke from her blunt.

"Ya'll know that nigga ain't coming down here. He rather take that bullshit from her than to risk coming down here, piss us off and risk us not only spilling *all* his business but stomping a mutt hole in his bitch. So ya'll ain't gotta worry about that one. On the other hand, that bitch feel like she got something to prove so *she* might try to come and step to you," she said, looking towards Mystic.

"And she gone get her ass beat! That bitch look like a man and I'm gone beat her ass like one!" Breeze snapped, yelling her message loud enough for his wife to hear.

Mystic knew the outcome of any of this couldn't be good. She was on probation and couldn't afford to get into trouble. No matter the ending, it was clear that things would never be the same between her and Spider.

Spider snatched his wife by her arm, spun her around and grabbed her in the collar of her shirt and everyone standing in front of 5954 braced themselves for a battle but it didn't come; not with them anyway. Spider's wife reached back balled up her fist and hit Spider with a doozy across his face.

"Daaaammmmnnnn," Harvey yelled across the street.

Chuckles echoed through the crowd.

Spider, trying his best not to put his hands on her, continued to grab her and hold her.

The hood watched as this spectacle continued for what seemed like hours. Spider stood his ground for Mystic. No matter how upset he was at what Mystic had done, he could never bring himself hurt her in that way.

His wife he could handle. This wasn't the first time and it definitely wouldn't be the last time she acted a damn fool. So her clowning was nothing new to him.

Realizing that she was fighting a losing battle, his wife finally retreated in the fight but not the war. As she began walking back across the street, she topped to yell one last thing Mystic's way.

"You want him bitch, you can have that muthafucka cause I don't need him! Bring yo' ass around the corner and get his shit cause its finna be in the muthafuckin' front yard!"

Mystic waved her hand and proceeded to go back onto the porch. Cocamo yelled behind her.

"This the drama you like? This the stupid shit you wanna deal with the next 21 years plus?"

"Drama seems to work for you!" she spat back, nodding towards the porch that now held Tee-Tee standing at top of the steps. Cocamo bit the inside of his jaw as he watched her walk up the steps and take a seat back on the ledge of the porch.

Things were becoming too crazy on the block; emotions, feelings and tensions were running high. No one knew what to do or what to expect but as Cocamo walked back over to his house, he looked up the steps at Tee-Tee and then glanced over at Mystic wiping her eyes. He told himself, something had to give and quick!

Chapter Eight

Man walked into the F & G Liquor Store with Breeze closely behind, walked over to the cooler, got a 24oz. can of Bud Light and headed for the aisle that held the item he came for, sandwich bags. Man needed to get his cush on the streets to his customers. As he turned down Aisle B, he ran smack dab into Spider and Tank.

Man exchanged pleasantries with Tank and when he made eye contact with Spider, Spider held out his hand for some dap as if this was just another ordinary meeting between the two of them. However Man, wasn't really in the receptive mood. He was still fuming over the scene they had just transpired on the block.

"What it do homeboy?" Spider asked him, popping Man on the chest with the back of his hand. "You see that shit up there? Man, she be on some ole crazy shit sometimes but it's all good. I don't trip off all that drama. I let that shit roll off me like sweat dripping off my balls.

Man looked at Spider like he had lost his damn mind. It wasn't that he had any personal beef with Spider. They were by all means cool from day one. Man just couldn't stand it when niggah's tried to act like they were top-notch players yet handled their business like lames.

It was no secret that Man didn't think Mystic should be dealing with Spider but he tried his best to stay out of the way. Normally, if it didn't directly interfere with his product, his way of life or his money, Man kept his nose out of other folks business and he expected them to do the same concerning his... unless it had something to do with someone he cared for and this situation fit that bill.

He gave Spider his dap but he also took the opportunity to speak his mind.

"All good? Niggah that shit up there just let me know you ain't handling yo' business like you running around here stunning like you are. You knew this had to happen eventually, the shit was too muthafuckin' close to home. You should have had a stronger grip on that handle, as in *handling* yo' business. That bullshit could've went a whole different way and kicked off a lot of static and shit."

Spider stepped back on his left leg and gave Man a look as if to say, "You know me better than that nigga."

"Seriously niggah? Do you really think I was gone let something happen to that girl?"

"*That girl?*" Breeze stepped in aggressively. "Oh so you in yo' feelings and now she just, *that girl?* Nigga that girl is my lil' sister and *I* wasn't gone let nothing happen to her. If yo' broad would've come down there trippin', she was gonna get her as whipped!"

Spider looked to Breeze, eye brows raised and chuckled.

"It wasn't gone be none of that. I know my folks so I know what she will and won't do."

"Yeah well, keep kicking a dog while he's down and eventually his ass is gone bite back. All I'm saying is you better tame yo' bitch when she do cause if not, I'm gone put her ass to sleep."

"I know you bout-it-bout-it Breeze but all that ain't gone be necessary. Me and you, we good. I care for your sister more than you think I do and I ain't gone let nothing happen to her whether we into it or not."

"Yeah well, you just better make sure it stays that way cause if anybody try to hurt her or that baby she carrying it's going down and you and I ain't gone be good no more, please believe."

As Breeze flung her hands in the air, ranting and raving about this and that, Spider focused in on what he thought he had just heard.

Baby? What the fuck?

Spider ran his index finger and his thumb down the sides of his chin as he pondered the thought.

Could it be?

"Baby?" he asked, looking back and forth between Breeze and Man.

Man chuckled to himself.

This nigga ain't got a clue.

Before Breeze could respond any further, Prez walked into the store, walked up behind Spider and touched him on the shoulder. Breeze cut her eyes to Man as soon as she saw Prez.

Spider hadn't seen Prez since they had the argument on the porch over Mystic. They had spoken a few times on the phone concerning business but things definitely weren't the same between them. Long gone were the days of fric-n-frac, hanging on the block or kicking it at the clubs together. All that was left to hold them in each other's world was their mutual love of the grind and money. Trust and loyalty would always be an issue between the two of them.

"What up pot'na, I just left from around the way. I been calling yo' ass for three days and you ain't hit me back so I came through to see what's good?"

Spider reached across Man and grabbed a box of sandwich bags.

"Shit it's been madness going on around these ways, you know that," he said, holding up the box. "I'm just now getting shit back on track."

"Yeah well, yo' track might wanna lead back to the crib cause yo' folks is up there like straight up buggin'."

Prez spoke to Man and Breeze but neither of them responded. Man shook the scene walking past Spider and bumping Prez along the way. Spider grabbed Breeze on the arm.

"I need to holla at you."

Man pulled Breeze away as he looked Spider up and down.

"Get yo' own 411 nigga and handle yo' business. We ain't 'bout to get caught up in no more of yo' drama."

Spider smirked at Man's statement but he could do nothing but honor it. It wasn't their mess, it was his and he would be sure to do just that.

Man glanced at Prez as he and Breeze stood in the checkout line. He thought back to the night he had gone to pick up Mystic at the gas station. The look on her face was one he would never forget. He had only seen that level of fear on someone's face once before and that was his sister's. Prez had been on his list of things to do every since that night and what Breeze was about to tell him would bump him up to the top.

"I can't stand that muthafucka," she spat out as she paid for their items. "He is such a fucking bastard!"

Man knew Mystic hadn't told Breeze about the park incident so he knew she had to be speaking about something else.

"Why you say that?"

"He be on bullshit all the time. I saw his ass downtown one day while I was at Union Station. I was on the bus stop heading to the crib when he pulled up on me and asked me if I needed a ride. I didn't trip off it cause you know I'm thinking, *that's Prez,* from the block. Then I get in the car, we riding and shit, we ain't get five damn blocks before this nigga gets to talking about stopping at his house to get a sack he gotta deliver to somebody.

So I'm like cool, whatever. We get to his crib, he fire up with me and shit. Before I knew it this nigga asking me for some head, for a punk ass blunt? I told that nigga if I go down there, I'm coming back up with that limp muthafucka between my teeth and unattached to yo' balls! Fuckin' pervert!"

Man bit down on the inside of his jaw as Breeze finished her story on their way to the jeep.

"When was this?" he asked her, watching Prez get in get into his champagne colored Cadillac.

He lit up his blunt and grabbed his phone from its holster. As he inhaled the smoke from his herbs, he sent a text message to his cousin Sheena who was a supervisor at the DMV.

"This was earlier this year when I still in school but I ain't fucked with his ass since. Trying to speak and shit. He got jokes."

Man was irritated with Prez even more. Not only did he put Mystic out in the dark, set her up to be robbed but he had tried the same thing with Breeze also. To Man, Prez stepping to Breeze was like Prez disrespecting him. It wasn't a nigga that graced the hood with his presence that didn't know that Breeze belonged to him and that he would not tolerate.

Man kept his thoughts to himself as he tilted his head to the side and toyed with the smoke coming from his lips. He looked down at his phone and retrieved the text message his cousin had returned to him. He smiled at the contents as he started the Jeep wrangler and pulled off the F&G lot. His list would soon be shorter, and he was definitely looking forward to that.

As Man rounded the corner onto Riverview, Breeze rubbed her hand down his thigh.

"Ooooooo, this my shit," she said, turning up the radio.

"...If I wasn't married to the streets it would be you. Yo' lips is what makes you so cute. Love when you polk yo' mouth when you mad too. Save yo' number in my phone under Lil' Boo. Like yo' sex but mo' in love with what you do..."

Breeze leaned over and whispered in Man's ear as he turned onto Harney.

"Don't stop, keep driving."

Breeze ran her fingers up Man's thigh and grabbed the bulge between his legs. Breeze loved the size of Man's jimmy, the feel of its multi-colored skin in her hands and the way his body responded to her touch.

She began to stroke Man's jimmy as he inhaled his blunt, trying to stay focused on the road ahead.

"...*Turn me on how you stare at me when we through. When you give it to me I don't wanna turn you lose. Scared to moan round you so all I can say is ooohhh...*"

The jeep turned right at Schulte as Breeze wet the tip of his jimmy with her tongue. She felt the car jerk and she smiled to herself. Slowly she inched his oversized jimmy inside her jaws until she felt it touch the back of her throat. Loosely she bobbed her head up and down against his skin, wetting it with her jaws and blowing a cool breeze against it.

When Man came to the stop sign a Park Lane and Schulte, Breeze used the opportunity to massage his jimmy with force. She tightened her grip and used her jaw muscles to pull on his skin with a vengeance. Man had trouble keeping his foot on the pedal and the jeep lunged forward out into the cross walk. Man grabbed her head and squeezed the back of her neck.

"...*My favorite panties are yours, the ones that's see through. Ones with the pink trim on 'em and they light blue...*"

Breeze felt Man's jimmy continue to stiffen as the jeep slowly pulled away from the stop sign. She swished the tongue around in her mouth, gathering her slob before holding her breath and sliding the wetness down his vessel. Man was in heaven.

"...*Speaking for the goon's, thank God for making you...*"

Breeze inhaled a deep breath and let her jaws loosely glide up and down his skin. The wind from her mouth drove him crazy. She felt the vein along the back of his jimmy begin to bulge and throb. She knew her desired outcome was near. She wanted to see if he could stay in control of the jeep as he let it loose and as the jeep turned right onto West Florissant, she would soon find out.

Breeze wrapped her hand around the base of his shaft and as her hand worked the bottom her lips worked the top, meeting joyfully in the middle. The tag team was about to make Man lose his mind. His left hand gripped the steering wheel, his right hand gripped her tighter around the neck and his legs did their best not to go numb. The jeep swirled in the lane to the right and Man tried his best to jerk it back into the left.

Breeze worked the muscles in her wrist and jaws harder until she brought Man to a peak so strong he had to pull the jeep off the road. His legs tightened, his foot was paralyzed on the brake and his jimmy was rock solid.

His moans became louder, his grip damn near a death hold and the tip of his jimmy erupted like a fire hydrant. His juices shooting into her mouth so strongly that Man felt lightheaded.

"...Buss it baby, is what I call you..."

Breeze gathered every drop of his juices, smiled and rose up from his lap and wiped the corners of her mouth.

"Shit, let me hit that blunt Boo," she told him, looking at the aftershocks of her work and loving it.

This was the other side of Breeze that Man loved. The confidant shit talking side of her. This was why he'd chosen her. She had what it took to keep him coming back.

"You made me drop that muthafucka out the window back on Schulte."

"Ump, I must be on my game baby! Anytime I make yo' ass drop a blunt I handled my shit! That's for making me wait on yo' ass all last night!"

"Shit, well if that was punishment, I'm gone make you wait on a niggah every time!"

"Whatever niggah," Breeze said, holding out her hand for another Cigarillo.

Man wiped his face with the bottom of his t-shirt and put the jeep into gear. He reached down inside the center console to retrieve another blunt, lit it up and handed it to Breeze as he pulled off. When he made it in front of Breeze's house, he told Breeze that he'd be right back.

The dome Breeze had just given him was fire but as Man glanced over across the street and saw Prez standing with the rest of the gang, his mind quickly went back to handling his business.

"I'll be back shortly. I got to go see a man about a dog."

To Breeze that meant he would be out in the streets doing dirt. She simply climbed out the jeep and headed up the steps.

Man picked up his phone and looked at his text messages once again. As he pulled off from the curb, he dialed up one of his boys from the south side.

"I need that from you like now. Got a problem I need to solve."

Chapter Nine

Toi came running from the gangway between Punkin and Unc's house and onto the steps where Mystic was still sitting on the porch, thinking about all the drama that had just gone down. She was staring off up thw block waiting to catch another glance of the man she loved.

Yet on the low-low, she was also waiting to see exactly how long Cocamo was going to have Tee-Tee over. As much as she tried to play it off, it really bothered her that Tee-Tee was next door all this time. She knew deep inside that Cocamo would eventually patch things up with Tee-Tee and she knew she had to respect that. After all, hadn't she just declared her love for Spider to Cocamo's face not more than thirty minutes ago?

Cocamo had a right, she reasoned to fix things in his world just as much as she herself wanted to fix the broken pieces between her and Spider. The kiss they shared was different, special even but she had to put that in the back of her mind.

As her eyes searched the corner for Spider's truck, Toi burst up onto the steps waving her hands in a very animated way and talking a mile a minute.

"Girl, that niggah Spider's wife is around there buggin'! She is throwing that niggah's shit all over the front yard as we speak! Girl she is around there clowning, you hear me?"

"*Whhhaaatttt?*" Breeze said, standing in the doorway. "I just seen his janky ass at the store a little while ago. I told him as long as he kept his bitch on a leash we won't have no problems."

Breeze stepped out the door and high-fived Toi as Mystic nervously looked off to the corner. It truly hurt her heart that the man her heart longed for so badly, was going through so much drama because of her.

"Well, she around there having a serious *Waiting to Exhale* moment on that ass!"

Toi playfully placed her fist up to her mouth and began singing.

"Shiiittt, she not gone cry, she not gone cry, she not gone shed no tears," she cruned.

Mystic was not laughing at the jokes between Toi and Breeze. She and Spider wasn't even on speaking terms and so she couldn't even be there for him through all the madness. She could only imagine the things that was going through his mind.

I'm so sure he is regretting the day he ever fucked with me. I'm causing him so much pain but if he would just give me one chance to make it right, I know I can make him forget about all this. His wife, this block, everything and we can do us and start our own thing, our own family.

Everyone kept trying to tell Mystic how to feel, how not to feel, how to act or how not to act. Mystic loved Spider and she wanted him, plain and simple. The last man she loved betrayed her in the worst way and she truly felt that things would be different with Spider..

She had known her ex the majority of her life. Growing up together in the county area of St. Louis, she thought marrying him would bring her the stable home life she had always longed for coming up as a child. When he had entered the military and asked

Mystic to be his wife, she was overjoyed that she had finally found what she was looking for. She knew she'd married a man with strong family values, a good work ethic and a good sense of responsibility. It wasn't until later after the marrital bliss had worn off that she'd found out that he had one more thing, a habit.

He gambled away their means to survive paycheck after paycheck. Thankfully, they lived on base so their rent and utilities were provided for and Mystic tried to make up the difference with a job but his addiction had taken their finances by storm.

When he had first brought the check cashing scheme to Mystic she was adamant about not participating but the more money he lost, the more she and her newborn baby girl lost their quality of life. He had promised her that she would never get caught. He had someone on the inside to do all the dirty work he had assured her so Mystic finally relented and began her life of crime in the name of love and survival.

Little did her or her husband know, the insider had already been caught and was now working with the MP's (Military Police) in bringing down those who participated in the scheme.

Her husband was careful not to sign any of the checks nor go into the PX with Mystic when she presented one. For six months the authorities allowed Mystic to cash fraudulent checks as they were building a solid case against her. When they finally cuffed her, Mystic was devastated.

Her indictment came down and Mystic was released on bond but in a restricted environment and wasn't allowed to return home. The closer her trial date came, the more her husband began to distance himself from her. When Mystic was arrested she had had her baby girl with her in the store and so DFS (Division of

Family Services) was called. Her daughter was eventually allowed to return home with her husband.

When her trial date arrived, it had been nine months since Mystic had physically been living under the same roof with her husband. She looked around the courtroom to find her daughter joyfully bouncing on her father's lap. Her joy was short lived as she also noticed a pretty younger looking woman sitting cozily next to her husband.

Mystic would later find that the relationship between her husband and the woman had been going on much longer than she had been in her legal situation. Mystic knew that his adultery also played a major role in the way he had taken the stand and protected his freedom by denying any knowledge of a check cashing scheme or that he knew Mystic had been passing bad checks. Mystic was devastated and the fact that he was raising her daughter with his new woman made things even worse.

She now understood the short visits to the YWCA to visit her and the excuses of why he could never bring her daughter to see her. Things got worse once Mystic was sentenced. He sent a few pictures of her babygirl here and there but could never seem to find the time to bring her daqughter the short 300 miles to visit her.

Mystic had vowed to herself that one day she would get her daughter back someday and make him pay for putting her through hell. All the pain he had put her through had made her a little wishy-washy towards love and Mystic had told herself she would never allow herself to love another man, especially one who wasn't strong enough to have her back. That all changed the moment she laid eyes on Spider. She wanted him more than she'd ever wanted anything and the fact that she was now carrying his child made her need for him that much stronger.

Her sister often joked that Spider had "turned her out," and for the most part, Mystic would agree with that. Spider had opened her up to a whole new life in the 'hood and she wanted to hold on to it all.

"There his ass go right there," Toi shouted.

Mystic quickly wiped her eyes and looked anxiously across the street as the Suburban came flying around the corner, system beating just like any other ordinary day. As the truck made a u-turn and backed up along the side of Get Down's house, Mystic stood up from her seat.

She stood there biting the inside of her lip. She knew that if she ever had a moment to take a chance with him, this was it and she wasn't going to let it pass her by. It was now or never.

Mystic fixed her clothes and walked down the steps to the chuckles and snickers of Toi and Breeze and waited for Spider to exit his truck.

"This Bitch just don't learn," Breeze snapped, shaking her head in disgust.

As Spider emerged from the truck, he looked across the street at Mystic, standing there. He fought the urge to go over to her. He looked at her face and once again his heart divided in two. Apart of him missed her terribly and didn't mind going through the drama for her because he knew deep down that Mystic would have his back whenever he needed her to. After all, she still held the secret that could send him to prison for the rest of his life. With all the mess that she had endured over the last few weeks for him, she hadn't told a soul.

To Spider, that meant a lot. For that reason alone, he felt the responsibility to at least calm things down between them. That plus he needed to know if what he thought he heard Breeze say in the store earlier was correct or not.

Mystic waved across the street and Spider nodded his head to her. He closed the back door to the truck and slowly began to walk towards her. Mystic got so nervous as she watched him cross the street. There was so much she had been waiting to say to him but now that they would finally be face to face, words escaped her. She didn't know where to begin.

She kept her eyes looking downward to the ground below as she twisted her fingers together. When she opened her mouth to speak her words came out almost in a whisper.

"Umm I just wanted to say that... that I'm really sorry that you gotta deal with all this with everything else you've been going through. Especially the things you're dealing with because of me. I know..."

"Look at me mommy," he interrupted. "Lift yo' head up and look at me."

Mystic hesitantly raised her eyes to him.

"When I first got with you, I told you never had to worry about nothin' as long as you with me, right? I kept it 100 with you even after you found out about my situation, did I not? When I said I wasn't gone let nothin' happen to you. I meant that.

I wasn't gone let her come down here and try to put her hands on you. I don't care if we into or not, just cause we ain't fuckin' with each other right now don't mean my word don't hold true."

Mystic gave a half-hearted smile. His words poured over her soul like cold water soothing her thirst on a hot summer's day. At that moment hearing him say those things to her lifted alot of the burdens from her shoulders.

Staring into his eyes, she now believed with more certainty than ever that their relationship could survive what they were going through and in time, things would be better for them and the child they shared.

"I really am sorry. I'd like a chance to explain everything. It was not how it..."

"I don't wanna talk about that shit right now. I just came to make sure you were good after all that shit went down today. I got too much other shit on my mind fo' all that other shit right now."

Mystic understood that and she relented to what he said but there was one thing she had to know.

"Can I ask you a question then? Please just answer me this one thing?" she said, her eyes pleading with his. "Do you believe me when I say that I love you?"

Spider looked at her and wanted so badly to pull her into his arms and hold her but he couldn't. He just didn't know how to force the rules of the game out of his head long enough to see the mistake he was making by letting this go on as long as he had.

"This ain't about love. And I told you I don't wanna talk about this right now. Now, what I wanna ask *u* about is something I heard a little bird talking about earlier."

Spider stepped closer to her and looked her directly in her eyes. He wanted to grab her so bad but instead he just looked up the way.

"Is there something you wanna tell me?"

Mystic looked up at him curiously. She didn't know exactly what he was referring to and she didn't want to say anything to put her foot in her mouth. As far as she knew, the news of her pregnancy went no further than those closest to her. She was hoping it wasn't anything else to do with Prez or Remo.

"Like what?" she asked him.

"Like why you been feeling..."

He was interrupted mid-sentence by an all white van pulling up behind his truck across the street with big black letters that read, *St. Louis Department of Health*. Usually when this van pulled up on the block, the city was looking for someone who had been reported for spreading some type of Venereal Disease. No one wanted to be the recipient of a knock at the door from the crew occupying this van.

Mystic and Spider watched as the two man crew jumped out the van, walked around to the back and opened its' doors. One of the men pulled out a manual wheelchair from the back of the van, sat it on the ground and opened it up. They crossed the street and began walking towards a wheelchair bound Kelvin James.

Kelvin was an old school player that had been in the Walnut Park neighborhood for over 20 plus years. Out of those years, he had been in a wheelchair for twelve after being involved in a car crash running from the police.

Every since Mystic and Spider could remember, Kelvin could be seen on any given day, riding up and down the block in his motorized wheelchair. That was about to change.

The block watched in shock as the two men walked up to Kelvin, strong armed out of his motorized chair and placed him in his new manual wheelchair. They business very quietly then walked back across the street, placed the wheelchair back into the van, walked around to the front, go it and drove off.

No one wanted to laugh in his face but the scene was too hilarious to hold it in.

"What the fuck?" Breeze said, laughing.

Everyone out on the block began to chuckle in disbelief. They had never seen anything like that before, not even on TV. Spider and Mystic couldn't help but laugh as well.

"No this niggah did not just get his wheelchair repo'ed. That some shit fo' You Tube! Who does that shit?" he said, laughing beside Mystic.

It was nice to laugh together again. It seemed as if it has been forever. Mystic wanted this moment to last forever as they continued to bust a gut watching him manually push himself down the block in embarassment.

Before they knew it, they were touching each other and smiling at each other. Spider looked at Mystic and rubbed her cheek.

"I been missin' you Mommy."

Mystic looked at him and felt a tear began to well up in her eye.

"I've been missing you too; oh so much."

"Maybe you should stay the night at the hotel tonight so we can talk about this shit. Maybe it is about that time," he told her, waving off Prez, who was calling for him to come over across the street.

Mystic felt her heart burst with joy. *Would she*? Nothing but death could keep her from being with the man she loved for the night.

"I'll hit u later," he told her as he walked back across the street. "Oh and we will talk about that question I started."

Mystic was overjoyed that she would finally have the opportunity to explain her side of the story and make things right with her man. Maybe this would be the perfect night to share with him her secret. After a night of talking and making love, it would be the perfect way to end the night by telling him about the love child they now shared together.

As Mystic turned to go back in the house she looked over to find Cocamo standing on the front porch smoking a cigarette. As she bounced up the steps, she tried not to look over at him.

He released a hail of smoke and snickered.

"I guess I ain't the only one who drama seems to work for, huh?"

With that he turned around, walked back into his house and slammed the door. Mystic shook her head. She didn't care at that moment what anybody had to say. She was on cloud nine and there was nothing no one could say or do to bring her down. She was about to have the night of her dreams with the man of her dreams. Come morning, everything would be right... or so she thought.

Chapter Ten

Tee-Tee lay across the couch staring up at the ceiling. She smiled at the thought of her and Cocamo together. If she hadn't been present the night all the drama went down she would have never known that they were into it just 24 hours ago. The way they made love seemed as if the chemistry had never left.

Tee-Tee was elated at the thought that Cocamo mentioned having a baby with her. To her, that was the ultimate show of affection a man could give towards a woman. She wished that moment could last forever. It was the first time that Cocamo had gone up inside her raw without protection. She didn't think anyone could understand the significance of that. A man like him, a womanizer in most eyes, never let himself slip up like that; so for him to blatantly go up inside of her raw, she knew that he had meant what he said to her and it was not just uttered in a moment of passion.

It was so easy for Tee-Tee to imagine a life with him now, equip with everything she had ever wanted. She knew for sure that Cocamo without a doubt could provide for her every need.

He was a hustler by nature and so was she. Whatever he couldn't bring in, she could. With Big Slug now out of the way, Tee-Tee had the fantasy of her and her man ruling the streets of Walnut Park together... Bonnie and Clyde, 'hood style.

The idea of lying next to the man she loved night after night, watching him sleep, feeling his body next to hers was unimagineable to her. There were so many times after that night after all that drama that Tee-Tee had thought this night would never come again and now that she had another chance she wouldn't let anything or anyone come between her and what she wanted.

Tee-Tee thought back to Lil Curtis and thought of how happy he would be for her. Only he had known her true feelings for Cocamo and how he had changed her world. For Tee-Tee to value someone over the grind and her love for the all mighty dollar, Lil Curtis knew Cocamo had to be special to her.

Tee-Tee missed her friend so much. After all, it was Lil Curtis that had sealed the deal between her and Cocamo. If he hadn't taken her purse to Cocamo when she'd gotten locked up, their relationship probably wouldn't have gone past that one night stand.

She closed her eyes and dreamed beautiful thoughts of Cocamo rubbing on her swollen stomach, kissing her softly on the back of her neck and telling her how much he loved her. She couldn't contain the excitement. She really had no one else to share her news with since Lil Curtis was now gone. There was no way her mom would take the news lightly since she already stayed on Tee-Tee's back about spending so much time in the streets and away from the child she already had but this would be different. Her first child had come unwanted but loved.

Her baby's father was a dead beat. She had run across him him one night in the *My Way* lounge. She had gone to the lounge to deliver some product to a customer and while she was waiting for him, she sat down at the bar to have a drink.

When the nice looking older gentlemen sat down beside her and began to strike up a conversation, Tee-Tee obliged him and accepted his offer to buy her a drink which eventually led to a night cap

It wasn't until she awoke the next morning and her hangover had worn off that she found out about wifey and his six children he told her he had to get home too. She had never heard from him again.

A baby with someone like Cocamo would be different. It would put her in a class all to herself. It would tell the hood that she had accomplished something that was impossible to the rest of them, she had captured his heart.

Tee-Tee grabbed her cell phone from the table and flipped it open, hit her contacts and pressed the down arrow until it rested on the number she wanted to call.

They weren't the best of friends but they weren't enemies either. They both shared a lot of similarities that made them associates on the block. They had both done time in prison, they both had a daughter and above all, they both was in love with men both complicated in nature. One was carrying her man's child and the other was hoping to soon be able to do the same.

Mystic looked down at the phone when she saw Tee-Tee's number come across her screen. They hadn't spoken in a while at least not over the phone. When Mystic had arrived back on the block, Tee-Tee had made it her business to introduce herself to Mystic.

Despite what she did in the streets, Tee-Tee was a mother and she understood how Mystic felt being away from her little girl. Tee-Tee had told her to call her if she ever wanted to talk to someone who understood what it was like to be locked away and the transition you had to make coming back out into the free world.

Although Mystic had never felt the need to discuss either topic with her, she did appreciate the gesture. Now, she was looking at her phone, listening to the voice of a woman who had just spent the day with the man that Mystic herself had just shared a very intimate moment with earlier that day.

Mystic wasn't sure if Tee-Tee's call had anything to do with Cocamo but she figured it had too.

Maybe she overheard one of the exchanges we had earlier or caught the sarcasm in some of the things we said. I don't know but I do know one thing, I'm not down for another woman calling herself checking me over her man today. This shit is really starting to get on my nerves.

"So what's up girl," Mystic asked her curiously. "What's going on?"

"Nothing much girl. I know we ain't chatted in a bit but I was just hitting you up to see what good with you."

Mystic frowned as she looked down at the phone. Now she knew that this call was some bullshit.

"Look Tee, it's been a long ass day and I..."

"I know it has and I'm gone be one hundred with you Mystic. I know this call is kinda out the way but I need to holla at you about something... well someone."

She paused and Mystic got ready to unload on her if she came at her cross in anyway concerning Cocamo.

"It's about Coco. The reason I called you is cause I thought you of all people could understand what I'm about to say given yo' situation with 'ole boy."

Mystic looked down at the phone once again and wondered what Tee-Tee could possibly know about her situation with Spider. This was the second time that day that someone had asked her about a situation. She was starting to wonder how the hood knew more than it was supposed to and Tee-Tee was about to confirm it.

"I know you must be excited about having a baby, especially after everything that went down with your daughter."

"Who told you that I was having a baby?"

"Girl boo! You know you can't keep nothing quiet in the 'hood. Don't nothing stay a secret to long around here, especially gossip. So anyways, I mean, I'm happy for you and all that but I wanted to get your thoughts or something along those same lines."

Mystic ears perked, her eyebrows raised in surprise.

Damn shame these folks can't keep they mouths shut and what she mean something along those lines?

To Mystic's distaste, Tee-Tee began to go on and on in detail about the time she'd spent with Cocamo earlier in the day. She held nothing back as she described the way he forced his way inside her and how he'd made her cum at gunpoint.

Mystic closed her eyes as Tee-Tee talked and imagined everything she was saying. Mystic already knew the feel of his lips and while what she reflected on turned her on, it pissed her off at the same time.

Why should she care though? Was she herself not waiting on phone call from her own man, coming to pick her up and take her to the hotel where they themselves would soon be making love? Yet even though Mystic was looking forward to spending the night with Spider, thoughts of Cocamo forced their way back into her mind, constantly since their lips had touched. Now here she was listening to another woman talk about how she'd experienced the very thing with him, Mystic could only dream of.

Nothing however could prepare her for what Tee-Tee was about to say to her next.

"Girl this niggah was going so hamm on me, all up in my guts when he leaned into my ear and said that my baby should have been his. Girl I couldn't believe it! At first I'm like, *what the fuck is this niggah on* cause my daughter is damn near four. But then he said it again and I'm like o-m-g, this niggah is asking me to have his baby!"

What? Mystic screamed within herself. *I know this bitch is lyin'! After all that shit he sat at the restaurant and said to me about bringing a baby into the world against a man's will and shit? I know he didn't ask her no shit like that*

After Tee-Tee continued to talk, Mystic had to accept it as the truth. Cocamo wanted her to have his baby. It came directly from his mouth and maybe what he'd said to her at the resturaunt was out of anger at his situation with Tee-Tee. Now that they had made up, he felt differently.

Then why was he still snapping on me when he saw me talking to Spider, knowing he had just got done fuckin' this girl? Boy niggah's ain't shit! I thought he was real! I can't believe him!

Mystic bit down on the inside of her lip, fuming at what she'd heard.

Any thoughts she'd had of being with Cocamo had now gone out the window and in a way she was glad. Her life, she tried to reason, needed to be all about her, Spider and the child unlike Tee-Tee's wishful thinking, she was definitely about to have.

Mystic lied and told Tee-Tee that she was glad that things were working out between her and Cocamo. Then she quickly made an excuse to get off the line and hung up.

Mystic closed her phone and threw it down on the bed. She couldn't believe Cocamo. All the things he'd said to her she had taken to heart only to find out it was all a lie. Mystic shook her head. She felt like a fool. She rose up off the bed as her cell phone rang again. She grabbed it from the bed, flipped it open and was relieved to hear Spider' voice on the other end.

"You packed cause I'm finna pull up."

"Yes," she replied.

"Come on out."

Mystic straightened her bed, grabbed her overnight bag from the floor and headed out the door.

"It's good Coco, you ain't the only one gettin' yo' freak on tonight and getting yo' shit right. So you wanna her to have yo' baby huh? It's all good, the hell with you."

Mystic walked up the steps to the front room and out the door determined to put Cocamo out of her mind for good and replace the thoughts of him with redeeming love for Spider.

What Mystic didn't know was that by the end of the night, thoughts of Cocamo would be the least of her worries.

Chapter Eleven

Mystic placed her bag down on the full sized bed in front of her and turned to find Spider standing directly in front of her. He looked so damn sexy to her. Dressed in her favorite NBA Lakers throwback jersey, a pair of calf length blue jean shorts and flip flops. This was the outfit he was wearing the first day she'd seen him on the block when she got out the half-way house.

She could still remember sitting on the porch, talking to her sisters Punkin and Breeze about the women in the Half-way House when she looked up across the street at the Suburban pulling up to the corner of Mimika and Harney. The system was booming out T-Pain's, *In love wit' a Stripper.*

When he stepped out the truck he instantly drew Mystic's attention. She couldn't take her eyes off of him. All afternoon she wanted a closer look and when Breeze finally called him over to their house to buy a dub sac of weed from him, Mystic finally had her chance. When he stepped onto their porch, Mystic was putting Pixie braids in Breeze's hair.

"Damn niggah, why I always gotta call you ten times to get yo' ass to walk across the damn street? You don't be doin' that much that you can't walk 50 feet across the street."

"Why you always on me like that Breeze, you know I'm out here grinding twenty-four seven, three sixty-five. I know you gotta get yo' issue off Boo," he said, looking at Mystic standing behind Breeze's chair.

Mystic tried not to look at him but she could smell his cologne blowing in the wind and it was doing something crazy to her. Breeze noticed Spider staring at her little sister and introduced them.

"Umm, the baby girl huh? You don't look like no baby too me. You visiting or you staying here now?"

"Staying," Breeze answered for her.

Mystic shook her head, yes. Spider smirked at her. She was pretty to him and she definitely peeked his interest but at the moment his mind was on a money run he had to make. He knew with her right across the street, he'd eventually have time to see what she was all about.

Mystic watched him walk back across the street so arrogantly yet so appealing to her. She would have never thought that day that she would be standing here in front of him, not only in love with him but carrying his child. Yes, they had some problems but she had gotten her man back and she fully intended to take advantage of him being back in her life.

She felt so excited not only to be in his presence again but alone with him, one on one. There was so much for them to talk about but as she looked up into Spider's eyes and inhaled his intoxicating scent, she told herself that anything that they had to talk about could wait 'til later.

Spider looked down at the woman who had literally turned his would upside down. Yeah he had cheated over the years with a large volume of women. Some he even considered himself to be in a relationship with but this one, this one had gotten under his skin and made him feel ways he never thought he could feel about a woman, even his wife. She drove him crazy in both good and bad ways. From the moment he first saw her on the porch braiding her sister's hair, he knew she would be his but he never expected her to impact his world the way she had. He was use to playing the field, loving and leaving skeezers daily but after the first time his lips touched hers, he knew it wouldn't be the case with this one.

He was still very upset with her for everything that had gone down but he loved her for all she had done and withstood just to be with him.

He dropped his bag down next to her on the floor and scooted to within inches from her face. Mystic took a hard swallow filled with intimidation and desire. It had been weeks since Spider had touched her. The last time she had felt him inside her was the night he'd given her the diamond earrings after making her wait three days to him once he was released from jail. She still had them proudly in her ears.

She didn't know what to say to him. He had made it plain that he didn't want to talk about events that had transpired over the past few weeks so Mystic decided to wait until he brought it up. She would let him take the lead.

Spider ran his hands down Mystic's arms and pulled her close to him. It felt so good to have her that close to him. It gave him an instant hard on.

"I got some frustration built up inside me. What you gone do about it?"

"Take care of you, as always."

Mystic reached up to kiss him. She placed a soft kiss on his left cheek and slowly moved around to his lips. He was hesitant return her kiss and Mystic could feel the tightness of his lips. That didn't deter her though as she continued to greet his lips with moist, soft pecks until he could no longer fight the feeling he felt building inside of him.

Spider gripped Mystic around her lower back and pulled her into his arms as their tongues played around in naughty unison. Mystic let her body fall limp inside his arms. This was the man she loved and would try her best this night to make him remember how much he loved her too.

Spider brought his hand up to Mystic's right breast and firmly palmed it like a basketball player gripping his favorite ball. His hands felt so good to her and she made sure he knew it.

"I've missed you so damn much. It feels like forever since I've tasted these lips. Ooooh my body is on fire from your touch."

Spider fought hard to keep the images of another man touching his woman out his head. She'd told him that Remo's advances were unwanted but Spider wondered, really wondered if she had meant it.

"How bad did you miss me?"

"Hella daddy, I've been dreaming of you. I've been touching myself almost every day wishing I could feel you."

Mystic grabbed the back of Spider's neck and dug her nails into his back with her other hand. She felt Spider's jimmy respond and his hardness felt so good against her skin. She was soak and wet. Her Victoria Secret panties were sticking to her like glue.

Spider slid his hand down her stomach to her belt and unbuckled it. He unsnapped her shorts and put his hand down between her thighs.

"Hmm, you drippin' I see. Guess you did miss me. You ever get this wet for another niggah?"

Mystic knew where that was going and she refused to let it. She pulled her head back, looked him in the eyes and told him, no.

"You and you only turn me on this way baby," she lied to him.

No, Remo hadn't made her body moist because he disgusted her but with Cocamo's touch earlier that day; he made it flow in ways she could have never imagined. As the thought of him crossed her mind, she dug into Spider harder. For a split second, she wished it was Cocamo standing there with his arms around her but she quickly forced the thought from her mind as Tee-Tee's words rang loudly in her ear.

He wanna go half on a baby with me.

Mystic instantly got upset all over again and she pressed her body harder against Spider's. She would let her rage over Cocamo fuel the fire and ignite the desperation she felt to hold onto her man.

"I told you I belong to you. I wish I could make you feel what I feel. It's you baby, it's all about you."

Spider finally gave in and rushed her mouth with vengeance. Aggressively he pushed her shorts down over her hips and down towards the floor. He threw her back onto the bed and began undressing in front of her. His eyes never left hers as he pulled off his shorts and jersey. He had all kinds of rampant thoughts running through his mind. He had to accept that Remo had been inside of her but he was determined to fuck any trace of him from her body and his thoughts.

Spider grabbed her by the arms and pulled her up to him and off the bed.

"Turn around!" he barked.

He spun Mystic around, put his hand between her shoulder blades and pushed her toward onto the multi-colored flowered comforter. He slapped her on the side of her thigh and told her to put her knees up onto the edge of the bed.

He gripped his jimmy and pushed inside her with deadly force. Harder and harder he pounded, taking no mercy on her flesh. Mystic moaned louder and louder as Spider dug into her ass cheeks with his nails and continued to hammer away. He lifted her up off the bed, placing her feet onto the foor and bent her upper body down towards the carpet. Rock solid, Spider guided his jimmy back inside her and continued his mission.

Mystic felt light headed at the position and tried to grab a hold of the bed. Spider yanked her hand away and continued to slam down into her.

"You... you're.... ba... baby you... you hurting me," she screamed.

Good! I bet that niggah didn't hit these muthafuckin' corners I'm tagging.

Mystic bit down on her lip and bared her nails down into the cheap carpet. Her moans now turning to screams.

Spider barreled down and nestled his jimmy underneath her pelvic bone. His fingers gripping Mystic's ass cheeks so hard he could have drawn blood. His load of semen was full of so many emotions... love, hurt, rage, joy and anger. He loved her, he couldn't lie but he couldn't stand her for hurting him either.

"Feel that! Yea feel all that!" he told her, smacking her on the ass.

He pulled from inside and stood her up. When he turned her to face him, he noticed the tears falling from her eyes.

"What's wrong mommy?"

"You hurt me," Mystic said, sniffling and looking off at the wall. "Really, you hurt me."

She turned away and sat down on the bed, grabbing her stomach. Spider looked at her apologetically.

"Damn, my bad mommy, I wasn't trying to hurt you like that. I just wanted to remind you whose pussy this is. What's up though? Why you holding yo' stomach like that?" he asked, Breeze's words in his ears.

He stood back and looked at her strangely.

"I asked you earlier if you had something you wanted to tell me."

Spider sat down beside her and placed his arm around her. He took his other hand and put it underneath her chin. He lifted her face to his.

"We done from keeping shit from each other, right? I ain't trying to hear nothing else on the streets from another muthafucka, feel me?"

Mystic shook her head. She began twiddling her thumbs trying to think of the best way to say what she had to say.

"You're already going through so much. I don't wanna add to your problems."

"Don't do that, talk."

"I'm pregnant," she said, looking away from him. "I found out while you were locked up and I was trying to tell you the night we had fell out but you was so angry. We haven't been speaking since so I haven't been able to talk to you about it."

Spider looked at Mystic then to the door. He stood up and walked over to his bag. He reached down inside, pulled out his half-empty bottle of MD 20/20, opened it, took a swig and tried to take in what he had just heard.

This shit is retarded. Does the drama ever stop? Damn! This girl gone send me to my muthafuckin' grave with all this shit. First Prez, then Remo and now.... hold up...

Spider turned to Mystic and took another hard swallow of his liquor.

"No disrespect Mommy but how you know it's mine?"

Mystic was prepared for a lot of answers. She had braced herself for him to say a lot of things but she would have never expected him to ask her that question.

"What?" she said in a soft hurtful whisper.

"I mean, how can you be so sure? Keep it real now, I ain't the only one you been with now am I?"

Mystic's heart dropped down into her stomach. She couldn't believe he would say something like that to her.

"Why would you say that?" she said, running over to him.

Her eyes pleaded with him not to make this more than what it was. She loved him dearly and all she wanted was for him to hold her in his arms and say that he loved her too. That was not about to happen.

"What you mean why would I say that? I thought we were 'bout to keep it real up in this muthafucka, huh? The real is you did fuck that niggah Remo, right? What about him?"

"What about him?" she yelled back at him.

"Come on Mommy, you did give that niggah some pussy! The only question is did you make that niggah strap up? So why you acting like the notion is so off the muthafuckin' wall, yes or no?"

Mystic's eyes watered again and shook her head at him in disbelief.

How could he think like that? Don't he know I would never do that to him?

"Don't say that baby, this is your baby! I found out while you were locked up. There's no way I could be pregnant by anyone *but* you. You weren't gone a damn year or something! You were only gone for a week or so. Please stop this, please."

Mystic tried to walk over to him and hug him but he walked around her and sat down on the bed. He sat the bottle down onto the floor between his feet and dropped his head down into his hands. Mystic's heart was torn in two. She sat down on the bed beside him and grabbed his hand inside of hers.

"Spider baby I can assure you I am having *your* baby. I know things got a little fucked up okay? I know but baby look at me..."

She placed her hands on the sides of his face and turned him to face her. She leaned forward and placed her forehead against his.

"I'm carrying your seed baby. We, you and I, are gonna have a baby."

Spider pulled her hands away from his face.

"Even so... even if that's so, I can't have no baby with you. You think my wife gone go for that shit? You saw her out there clowning today and that's only cause she think I'm fucking you. What the fuck you think she gone do if she find out you say you pregnant? I told you when I got home from jail that sometimes you got to march to the beat of another muthafucka's drum when they know too much of yo' business. How she gone act knowing somebody is walking around this muthafucka with my baby?"

He paused, waving his hand in the air.

"And I thought you couldn't have no kids, what the fuck was up with that?"

"Umm hello, I got a Norplant after I had my baby and two years before I got locked up. That's been almost seven years ago and they only last for five! You do the math! And I thought after today that," she said, getting up.

"You thought what? I was gone pack up, leave my family and live happily ever after with you?"

Yes, that was what Mystic thought and she was overwhelmingly disappointed that he stood there telling her that it was not going to happen that way. Spider looked at her and saw the hurt in her face. This wasn't her fault alone he admitted to himself but it was no way he could go home to his wife and tell her another woman was carrying his child.

"Look Mommy, I'm sorry, I don't mean to hurt you, really I don't. I play out here in these streets all day, feel me? And yeah, sometimes I do my thang on the side. This here thing with you was way more than a hook was supposed to be. I got in deep with you and I don't blame that on you. That's something I will never regret either cause I love you but trust and believe I gotta go home. This here," he said pointing his finger back and forth between the two of them. "This here was all good until shit started getting twisted. Now it's a full blown mess and I gotta do what I gotta do to fix it and popping up with a kid ain't gone do it," he paused.

So the only thing I can tell you is to make an appointment at Family Planning and let's get it taken care of now."

Mystic couldn't believe her ears. Was he seriously asking her to get an abortion?

How could he ask me to do something like that? He knows my situation with my daughter. How could he say he love me and ask me to give up yet another child?

Punkin had told her, Cocamo had told her but most of all Man had told her that this day would come. When forced to choose between her and losing his home life, she would find that his love for her ran no further than her being the woman-on-the side. Over and over again they had warned her but Mystic had refused to listen. Now she was sitting on the bed, heartbroken and realizing that reality was a bitch.

They always go home girl, don't be stupid. Punkin words echoed in her ears.

They were all right it fact compounded the hurt she felt. She felt like such a fool to have loved him more than her common sense should have told her too. She couldn't go back and admit to them all that she was wrong about the way she was sure he felt about her. She had told them all that she was a big girl and that she could handle the game and all that came along with it.

"I don't want to have an abortion Spider; I want to have this baby. I wanna have this baby cause it's yours. Cause I love you and I'm begging you please not to do this."

She walked over to Spider continuing to plead with him to see things her way. As much as he cared for her, Spider couldn't allow himself to even entertain the thought. What had gone down today between him and his wife today wasn't abnormal to him. Spider knew he'd be back home in the morning or the next day. Coming back with news of a baby on the way was simply not an option.

"It can't happen Mommy. It just can't happen. Ain't know need in crying about it. You knew I was married so you knew the consequences. Look I can't do this with you right now. I got way too much other shit on my mind right now."

Mystic sat back in amazement. Was this the same man she had fallen in love with? It couldn't be she told herself. This couldn't be the same man that lay between her legs on so many occasions and told her how much he loved her.

"We'll talk about it some more tommorrow. Right now, I'm going to sleep."

With that he walked over to the bed, pulled back the cover, climbed in and turned his back to her. Mystic sat there for a moment realizing that this was no longer a fairytale. He wouldn't come around and that hurt her deeply but the fact that he didn't even want to discuss it hurt her even more. Yet she refused to believe that this was all there could be to their relationship.

Mystic lay back in the bed and scooted close to him. She rolled over and placed a kiss on his cheek.

"I really do love you baby," she told him.

"If you love me, you'll do what I asked you to do."

Mystic sighed, rolled over and turned off the light. Mystic felt the tears began to roll down her face once more. She tried to assure herself that in the morning, maybe after some much needed rest, he would see things differently. She was wrong.

Chapter Twelve

Cocamo sat on his couch smoking a blunt, blasting the sound system and playing Madden 11 on the PS3. He was waiting on Tee-Tee's arrival after he had texted her and told her that he needed to see her.

It was six thirty in the morning and Cocamo needed to get some things off his chest. He hadn't slept a wink that night and all he kept thinking about was seeing Tee-Tee standing in front of him talking about having his baby.

"What the fuck happened last night? I gotta quit fucking with that 'Tron. This shit is getting real retarded!"

Unc walked into the living room dressed in his navy blue bath robe and slippers, holding his coffee mug in one hand and a newly lit Newport in the other. He was carrying his round pillow cushion underneath his arm. He gingerly eased himself down on the black leather reclining chair and grabbed the ashtray off the coffee table.

"What it do Nephew, I see you had a busy day yesterday, huh?"

Cocamo snickered.

"What's all that about Unc? My day wasn't no busier than yours," he laughed. "Don't act like you wasn't cross the way gettin' it in old timer."

"Yeah, yeah... whatever Neph but at least mines is a lover, not a crazed maniac! Now I know you probably better than anybody, so for me to look up and see you walking up the steps and letting that woman come back up into this house tells me that you really got some deep ass feelings for this one. Especially after all the bullshit that went down and a bullet ending up in *my* ass!"

"It's crazy Unc. I saw her ass yesterday crying and shit. A niggah felt a lil' something in his chest for her, feel me? I know shit got twisted and she was on some bullshit at first with that niggah but Unc in her own way, she held me down cause she had the opportunity to handle her business many tears but instead she took the heat for me, so I felt a lil' sorry for her.

Then we up in here and that 'Tron kicked in and all hell broke loose. I went at her, hard. I'm asking this bitch all kinds of questions at gun point. Did you really think you could play me? Did you really think you was gone get this shit off, blazae blaz... I mean the more I spit at her, the more pissed off I got and I'm up in her face. I pulled my heat and put it up to her head."

Unc raised an eye brow at what his nephew had just told him.

"Yeah man, one second I was ready to knock her ass but in the next I was fucking her ass at gun point! Drunk and on some other shit."

Unc chuckled as he reached forward to put out his cigarette and retrieve the blunt from his nephew.

"I don't know what happened. The shit was just crazy all the way around. And the wild part is, the whole time I was digging up in her, I'm thinking about that cream next door. Being with her yesterday fucked with me more than I wanted to admit it to myself. But with her tied up in all that craziness with that gay ass niggah and all this bullshit I got going on, I figured it was better not to pursue that avenue. The shits been fucking with me though. So much that I was into my issue with her and Tee-Tee's raw. Now this bitch talking 'bout she wanna have my baby shit. That's definitely a no-no!"

Unc sipped his coffee and nodded his head.

"Nephew it is what it is. Sounds like you still got some unresolved issues with ole girl but you thinking about moving on with Mystic. Now you know I love Mystic like she my own kid. I done watched her damn near grow up on this block but right now she got her head up on cloud nine over that niggah Spider. Hell he came and picked her up late last night around 11:30 or something like that."

Cocamo smirked as he inhaled his blunt.

That niggah got her mind and gone with that muthafucka.

"For the life of me I can't understand what the fuck she sees in that niggah!"

"You ever thought that maybe she wondering the same thing about what the hell you see in ole girl," Unc responded.

"Whatever dude, that's some bullshit. That niggah don't mean her no muthafuckin' good. He don't give a shit about her. Now she wanna have his baby? Come on Unc man admit it, that's some lame shit," Cocamo said, rising up to go answer the door. "And how the fuck was you next door fuckin' yesterday with one good ass cheek?"

Cocamo laughed as he opened the front door.

"Fuck you Neph!" Unc spit back at him as he slowly pulled himself up from the chair. "Don't worry about my ass, it's yo' ass you better watch," he said looking to Tee-Tee as she entered the house.

Unc spoke to Tee-Tee as she walked inside the living room and then he excused himself from the room so that they could be alone. Unc had hoped that his nephew could see that messing with Tee-Tee could be poisonous to his life but Unc also knew all too well that matters of the heart could be very blinding sometimes.

Tee-Tee walked into the house and held up her hand for Cocamo to pass her the blunt.

"Damn, no hello? Where they do that shit at?" he said, pushing her.

Tee-Tee took the blunt from Cocamo's hand, stood in front of his face, inhaled the blunt and blew the smoke back directly in his face.

"Sup," she said handing him back the blunt. "So what you wanna see me about? You miss me all like that already?"

Cocamo chuckled and walked around her to the couch.

"You know that niggah Slug's wake today, ain't you going?"

Tee-Tee looked at him confusingly.

"Why would you ask me that? Why would I go to that niggah's wake?"

"Shit, why wouldn't you go is the question? You was his number one soldier, ready to do anything for him. Shit if you had anymore loyalty I wouldn't be standing here."

Tee-Tee grabbed her bag and waved her hand in the air. She knew the subject would come up again eventually but she didn't expect him to ask her over just to throw Big Slug's wake up in her face, not after last night. She had thought that they had made significant progress the night before.

"I see you in yo' feelings so I'm out. Don't call me over here just to talk shit to me. How you gone even come at me like that after last night? They say a drunk ain't shit! So you was just saying whatever just to get yo' rocks off? All that *have my baby* talk was just some bullshit, huh?"

Cocamo put out the roach in the ashtray on the table and walked over to Tee-Tee.

"What the fuck I look like having a baby with a muthafucka that just tried to kill me last week? Who the fuck does that Tee? Muthafucka's round here already looking at me like I'm crazy for even fucking with you think I would bring a kid into this madness?"

Tee-Tee shook her head and reached for the door knob.

Cocamo grabbed her hand.

"I ain't mean to say it like that. I really didn't."

He paused and turned her to face him.

"Look Tee come sit down fo' a minute."

They walked over to the couch and Tee-Tee sat her bag down beside her on the ledge. She looked at Cocamo and felt something very painful building up inside her. She really thought that this was the second chance she was hoping for. It wasn't that she didn't understand his position and she knew he had the right to heal at his own pace. Tee-Tee just wanted them to move past it and be able to let it go and after the previous night she was under the impression that that was exactly what had happened. She was wrong, very wrong.

"On the real, yesterday probably shouldn't have happened. No, not probably, I know it shouldn't have and if you keep it real with yo'self, you know it shouldn't have either. I was on that 'Tron and shit got a lil' crazy, this here...," he said, pointing back and forth between the two of them. "This shit just can't roll back to what it was Tee. It's some serious issues in the midst of all this shit. And I'm gone go so far as to say it ain't on you, it's on me. I shouldn't have gone there with you knowing how I felt about all this shit."

Tee-Tee shook her head in agreement. She couldn't do nothing but honor what he said and respect the fact that he kept it real with her.

Cocamo hit her on the side of her thigh.

"And I damn shol' should *not* have given you Mr. Good Dick!" he said laughing.

That got a smile out of Tee-Tee and kind of broke the tension of the situation.

"Whatever niggah."

"Seriously though, I ain't saying we can't work some shit out, I'm just saying a niggah need some time to figure out some things, feel me? I ain't got no beef wit' you mo' but shit ain't what it should be either, aight?"

Tee-Tee looked down at her lap and nodded her head.

"I feel you. So what now?" she asked him.

Cocamo lit up another blunt and handed it to her.

"I can't say. I mean, I'm gone do me and I'm gone be me, plain and simple. I'm sure you gone do the same. If we connect in the future, we connect. If not, it's all good. The biggest thing is that we good, right?"

Tee-Tee inhaled the blunt and nodded. As she blew out the smoke it was like exhaling a weight off her shoulders. At least he had assured her that there would be no more static between them and in time they may be able to work things out, slowly. She couldn't really ask for more than that given the circumstances.

"It's cool. I gotta admit, all this shit was a lil' wild. After all I do need to get my mind back on the grind. Get my money right and help take care of my niggah's family," she said, standing up.

"Speaking of, what you gone do about yo' product? You know you can always come work fo' me," he said, slapping her on the ass.

"Not no but hell no niggah! I'm done being a souljah, it's time for me to be a boss," she said walking towards the door. "Besides didn't you learn, you never mix business with pleasure and anything we do from here on out is strictly pleasure."

She turned and walked back to Cocamo and looked him directly in the eyes.

"My number ain't gone change. We can still play around whenever you get that feeling. As soon as you get an itch, call me and I'll come running to scratch it."

With that she placed a kiss on his lips and headed to the door.

Cocamo walked her out onto the porch and immediately frowned when he saw Spider's truck pulling up in front of Mystic's house. He stepped down onto the top step and watched as Mystic jumped out the passenger seat bag in hand. This was strange to him because usually he had the sickening pleasure of watching them drooling all over one another before she exited the truck but as his system bumped out Lyfe Jenning's, *Must Be Nice*, Mystic closed the door without so much as a word between the two of them.

"... Must be nice, having someone you don't have to show they exactly where it hurts. Must be nice, having someone you don't have to tell you don't wanna be alone..."

Tee-Tee spoke to Mystic as she headed up her steps but Mystic just kept walking. Tee-Tee shrugged her shoulders and continued on about her way. She turned to Cocamo before heading up the block and told him she would call him later.

When Mystic reached her front door she glanced over at Cocamo, back to Spider and then back to Cocamo. She then put her key in the door as she heard Spider cut down his system and speak to Cocamo. Cocamo half assed spoke and looked back to Mystic. He knew something was wrong.

"Guess yo' night ain't go so good huh?" he asked sarcastically.

Mystic was not in the mood for nobody's bullshit. Her heart was hurting and she just wanted to go inside and retreat to her room. She couldn't take one more, *I told you so.*

"Just leave me alone! I ain't felling this shit right now!" she screamed, plopping down on the ledge of the porch. She let the tears flow mostly because she just couldn't hold them in any longer. She didn't want him to see her cry but it couldn't be avoided.

Tee-Tee heard Mystic's outburst as she reached the tip of the alley and she looked back to see Cocamo jolting down the steps and across the grass. She didn't think too much of it at the time and she continued on her journey.

Cocamo sat down beside Mystic and put his arm around her waist.

"My bad, you know I be trippin' sometimes. I didn't mean to get you all upset."

"It ain't you," Mystic whimpered.

"The baby?"
Mystic sobbed as she shook her head.

He said I was a fool to think we could have a baby together and that he would ever leave home to be with me. And I know you told me but please, not now with the damn I told you so's."

Cocamo shook his head. Yes, he knew this was going to happen sooner or later but deep inside he wished Mystic could have avoided all this. He cared for her and he hated to see her hurt like that.

"Aey, come on next door, come on. Get away from all this for a lil' while. I mean I'm sure the last thing you wanna do is answer all the questions waiting fo' you on the other side of that door."

Mystic agreed as Cocamo grabbed her bag and walked her next door with his arm still tightly around her waist. It felt good around her and Mystic held on tight. Once inside, Cocamo placed her bag down on the floor beside the couch and told her to have a seat in the recliner. He went into his room and retrieved a blanket and pillow.

Mystic watched as he made her a pallet on the couch and told her to come get comfortable and rest for a while.

"You good, gone and kick back. I ain't gone let nobody fuck with you."

Through her tears she smiled within. She loved the way he seem to always take control of a situation and just with the things that came out of his mouth, he seem to always make it better.

He handed her the remote to the TV.

"Did the niggah feed you?

"No," she softly replied.

"Simp ass niggah," he whispered. "I'll be back in a sec, I gotta run to make. Just kick back and chill."

"As Cocamo walked around to the back side of the couch, he leaned down to her.

"It ain't worth it, feel me? I'm gone give you a minute to feel sorry for yo'self and then you need to shake that bullshit off. You got other things to worry about than that lame ass niggah."

Cocamo walked back to Unc's room and told him Mystic was on the couch resting. Unc looked at him confused.

"What happened to ole' girl?"

"You said to watch my ass," he laughed and closed the door. "I plan to Unc, I plan too."

Cocamo left and as he headed for the Schnucks on Jennings Station Road and West Florissant to get some groceries, he tried to make sense out of things. He didn't know what to make of the things that were happening around him. He had gone from the hood's biggest player to juggling his heart between two women in a matter of weeks.

He had love for Tee-Tee, he wouldn't deny that but he would never be sure if he could ever trust her again and that was monumental to Cocamo in his game. Mystic was simple to him, easy to love and be around. It didn't take much to please her. He didn't know what it was that was drawing him to her but he didn't fight it he just decided to let it flow.

When he returned home he found Mystic asleep on the couch. He made her some breakfast while listening to one of his favorite cds, the soundtrack to the *North Side Clit*. As *No Justice* flowed out a sick ass rap to the mellowing melody, Cocamo whipped up some bacon, eggs, grits and toast.

"*...From the bed to the floor, from the floor to the couch, non- stop in and out action til she tappin' on out. My body against her body like we LSG, the side effects will leave dehydrated like* *that xctasy. Caressing me with a look in her eyes oh so sweet, I had to keep her from seeing that weaker side of me…"*

When Mystic awoke to the plate he'd made for her she was stunned. Who would have thought a man like Cocamo could do his thing in the kitchen. Mystic smiled and thanked him. She couldn't believe her eyes. There was so much more to him than the hood knew. She was sure that there was another person in the hood that knew of his many talents and Mystic just didn't want to think about it or her.

Cocamo told her that he had business to attend to and that she was welcomed to stay for as long as she liked before he headed out the door. The scene was so sexy to her. The many sides of him were such a turn on. She especially like the fact that besides doing all these things for her and making her feel at home, he not once asked her what happened between her and Spider. She appreciated that more than anything.

Although the thought of lying wrapped in his cover all day inhaling his scent sounded so good to her, Mystic couldn't help but wonder if this was the same cover he had just laid with Tee-Tee moments before she arrived. She had already known they had made love the previous night and Mystic really didn't want to come between them getting their relationship back on track just because hers was going sour with Spider. Yes, she was attracted to Cocamo in ways she never thought was possible but she couldn't afford to fall for another man who was involved with someone else.

When she finished her breakfast, she placed her plate into the sink, folded his cover, placed it back onto his bed, grabbed her bag and left.

Chapter Thirteen

Mystic poked her head out the door to retrieve the mail for Punkin. She had just finished getting lectured by Breeze about hiding out in the house.

"You letting these niggah's control yo' every move. Okay so you got knocked up by a married man, so what! That shit happens every damn day. This ain't just on you, that's what you need to understand. Did you get yo 'self pregnant, no! That niggah laid down with you, dick naked and made a baby. He don't want no part of it, fuck him.

You move on, you raise yo' baby and you keep it pushing. One things fo' certain, you need to hit his ass where it hurt. He wanna act an ass, you act one too and get that child support. But aint no need in sitting up in this house rotting away. Now I know you caught up in yo' feelings but if you let that sexy muthafucka next door get by you, you crazy!"

Mystic looked at Breeze and shook her head. It really was nothing that went down in the hood that remained a secret.

"This niggah is checking fo' you and you carrying another niggah's baby? You better move yo' gear from being stuck on stupid and slide it up to getting' mines! Spider in the game yes, he showed you shit okay but this niggah is the total package and the biggest part, is that he single."

"He's not single, he still got shit going on with Tee-Tee," Mystic said trying to justify her feelings.

"And you care because what?" Punkin said coming into the kitchen. "What do I have to do to get you to figure this shit out.

Niggah's gone be niggah's Mystic plain and simple. You running around here looking for that *Young and the Restless* shit well this ain't it. The niggah's in the hood is loyal to one thing and one thing only, they money.

And you need to start figuring out how that loyalty can benefit you and that baby you carrying. Fuck all this falling in love shit! If you find it one day, whoopee but for now get yo' mind right and use yo' damn brain. The niggah want you! You know how bitches runnin' around here wishing they can say that? Spider made his choice and he made the right one."

Mystic looked at her and frowned. How could her own sister feel that way?

"Yeah he made the right one and I tell you why; that's his home Mystic. That's where all his responsibilities lie. He got a wife, kids and bills. What the fuck was he supposed to do? Now Breeze telling you to hit his ass up fo' support for just one kid; what about the five around there? You do the math. He did right. I ain't saying he couldn't have done it differently but he did what he had to do. Like Breeze said, Coco trying to get at you. What you got to lose cause I don't see a damn thang!"

Mystic hated to admit it but she knew in her heart that her sister's were right. It wasn't that he'd gone back home that pissed her off, it was the fact that he wanted her to abort her baby to hold on to a family he never acted like he gave a damn about before. Yet, his mind seemed to be made up and Mystic was tired of worrying about it.

When she stepped out to grab the mail, she saw Spider's truck pulling off from across the street. He floored it down to the front of her driveway and pulled in. Her stomach tied in knots as he let the window down.

"So you can't answer yo' muthafuckin' phone?"

Mystic lied and told him that she had been taking a nap when the truth was that when she saw his number flashing across the screen she just didn't feel like hearing him pressure her anymore. She could've never imagined things would get this way between the two of them. Some moments she felt it was better when they weren't speaking at all. At least then every word that came out of his mouth wasn't so damn hurtful.

Mystic was tired, tired of it all. There had been moments, she would admit, that she had thought about ending the pregnancy just to end all the problems and try to get back some normalcy to her life but Mystic had caved into the pressure of a man once before and it ended up costing her seven years of her life that she could never get back. To do that again was not an option for her. She wanted her child.

I'm tired of losing.

If Spider insisted on not being a part of her life or her child's life, as much as it hurt, she would have to let it be. She loved him yes, with all heart but Mystic needed to love herself and the child she was carrying inside of her more.

"Don't make me get out this muthafuckin' truck! I said come here!"

Mystic sighed, walked down the steps and over to his driver's side door.

"Look me in my face and tell me that what you texted me yesterday was on the money."

Mystic had gotten so irritated with the phone calls that she had texted him and lied to him, telling him that she had called and made an appointment to have the abortion done the following week.

"Don't you see how this will make this shit better fo' us Mommy? Shit can go back to the way it was before all this madness. Things is finally settling down around the corner and I'd rather just let the shit settle so we can go back to doing us. You miss me don't you?"

For the first time since she'd laid eyes on him, Mystic didn't really know the answer to that question and it frightened her. She found it so hard to believe that the man she was looking at was the same man she had fallen so in love with.

"Spider, tell me something. If none of this would have ever happened and I mean none of it… the jail thing, Remo, the pregnancy, where would we be? I mean like where would our future be heading?"

Spider looked off down the street and then back to her.

"I thought when I started fuckin' with you that you was the one. The one I could share my life with in a special way. I thought you'd never give me any problems and that I could groom you to be the woman I needed you to be. I needed you to be down with me and you were. But I shouldn't have thought that you could survive at this level of the game and that's my bad cause you still got some maturing to do. Not as a woman but as a woman who wants to be a part of this game and this lifestyle."

He touched her on her cheek as Mystic looked away.

"I can't walk away from my family and if you were the woman I thought you were you would never ask me too. Me and you... we can work as long as we have an understanding and everybody play their part and stay in their lane Mommy. You signed up fo' an understudy but now you hell bent on having the starring role. Shit just don't work like that Boo."

Mystic had refused to cry anymore. The situation was what it was and there was nothing she finally realized that she could do about it.

She nodded her head and began to back away from the door.

"Where you going? Gimme some of my sugah." He demanded, pulling her towards him by the bottom of her shirt.

Mystic gave him what he asked for just to get away from him before she ended up breaking down. For the first time his kiss repulsed her and she wanted to puke.

"I'll call you a lil' later aight and you better answer my call! I need some of that fo' it gets all bloody," he said, pinching her between her legs.

Mystic turned and began walking away as Cocamo pulled up into his driveway. She wasn't trying to run into him. She had been hiding from him since he'd made her breakfast. As Spider pulled out the driveway she tried to hurry up the steps before he exited his jeep and said anything to her.

As she reached the top step and headed for the door, he called out after her.

"What you runnin' fo'? You actin' funny?"

"No I'm not, why you say that?" she responded, walking over to the porch ledge over his driveway. She was now sitting right above his head.

"Shit I can't tell! A niggah cook you breakfast and try to be there fo' you and you just up and disappear. You start shittin' on him. Apparently you don't know who I am? I mean this Coco baby; what the fuck is all that about? That niggah got you on one like that?"

Mystic rolled her eyes.

"No, it didn't have nothing to do with him. I know exactly who you are and that's why I didn't wanna stop yo' flow. You got yo' thang working again with ole girl and I was respecting that plain and simple. That's all it was. I didn't wanna interfere with yawl's mating time since ya'll working on making babies and shit."

Cocamo laughed.

"Awww, you jealous?"

"No!" Mystic huffed.

Cocamo waved his hand and turned to walk back onto his porch. When he reached the door, he looked back over to Mystic entering her door.

"Wish you were… would've been so muthafuckin' sexy of you."

Mystic pounded her fist down inside her hand.

Ugghhh, what the fuck is wrong with these niggah's!

"What all that's supposed to mean? You got something to get off yo' chest, come on across the driveway."

"Well I do," she said, hopping down the steps, darting across the driveway and up his steps.

Cocamo opened the door and gestured for her to come inside. Mystic stepped inside and closed the door behind her. Cocamo walked over to the back of the couch, threw his keys down on the table beside him and told her to say what she came to say.

"You got the floor."

Mystic had second thoughts about what was on her mind but if she was ever going to stand on her own two feet and validate her emotions when it came to a man she figured that this was a good place to start.

"How is it that you can talk all this shit to me about bringing a baby in this world into drama and shit but you'll go off and consider having a baby with a bitch that wanted to hurt you just two damn weeks ago?"

Cocamo couldn't quite understand why Tee-Tee felt the need to share that with Mystic but he had a pretty good idea why. That or either Unc had been next door pillow talking with Punkin's gossiping ass again. Either way, he'd put an end to it later. Right now, it thought it was the cutest thing that Mystic cared so much.

"Who the fuck told you that?"

"Who else? Tee-Tee actually called and told me last night because she was so damn overjoyed and needed to share it with someone she thought would understand. She was so excited that her *Boo* wanted to go half on a baby with her," she said sarcastically. "Why do the rules apply to me but not to you?"

Cocamo walked into the kitchen to fix him a drink. He grabbed himself a shot of Patron and poured Mystic a glass of Apple juice.

"Now how the fuck does that sound? You know damn well I ain't having no baby with that girl," he said walking into the living room and handing her the glass of juice.

"Yeah right niggah, then why would she say that?"

"Cause while I was fuckin' the bitch last night, I told her that the baby should've been mine."

Mystic frowned and flicked him the finger.

"Exactly, why would you say that and she ain't pregnant?"

Cocamo walked over to her and stood within inches from her face. He looked her straight in the eyes, placed one arm around her waist, pulled her to him, placed his hand on her stomach and kissed her with so much force Mystic thought she'd have a coronary as fast as her heart began to beat. He tongued her down and Mystic couldn't catch her breath. When he released her he looked down his hand on her stomach.

"But you are."

Chapter Fourteen

Spider walked into the small two and a half bedroom brick home on Emma he shared with his wife, five children and two grandchildren. He sat down on the hunter green leather sofa and looked around the living room. It looked as if a tornado has blown through at full force. The everyday scene was one of the major reasons Spider stayed out in the streets so much. He could have easily handled his business from the comfort of his own home but he couldn't stand the constant noise, the filth and the bitching that would come along with that.

Being in the basement around the corner with Mystic gave him peace and solitude, Emma gave his security.

Spider sat back, took a swig of his Bud Light and thought back to a time when a then sixteen year old Kyrah's plump booty caught his eye as she was walking down Arsernal to catch the bus to get to school. Spider, four years her senior, was hypnotized by the bouncing of her cheeks and pulled his bronze '85 Cutlass over to the curve, rolled down his passenger side window and asked her if she needed a ride.

"I know you must be tired from carrying all that extra weight around."

Kyrah shook her head, no.

"They ain't that heavy. It just look like it. I forgot my bookbag in my locker yesterday. I'll be aight but thanks anyway."

Spider laughed.

"Lil' Momma I ain't talkin' about no books, I'm talkin' about them two dogeballs you got in the back of yo' pants."

Kyrah looked back at her butt and then back to him. She smiled at him and shook her head. She was used to the comments concerning her backside but she didn't mind, he was cute.

"What school you go to?"

"O'Fallon Tech," she answered.

"Get in," he told her reaching over to unlock the passenger side door.

"*Get in?* I don't know you like that and you shol' don't know me!"

"I've seen you around here before a few times," he lied. "And I promise you, I would never forget a body like that. My mom's stay over this way."

"Well how come you ain't even so much as asked me my name before now?"

Spider looked down and chuckled at her wit. He like that.

"Because I already know yo' name."

Kyrah finally stopped walking and turned to him, books clutched in her arms.

"What is it?" she asked.

"Mines," he said matter-of-factly. "Now you ready to go?"

Kyrah looked at him and laughed. She liked the way he had just put a claim on her. She could tell by car he was driving, all the gold around his neck, wrist and fingers that he was either a dope dealer or he had a really good job. In the hood she knew that it was probably the first one but as she climbed in the car and began to hold conversation with him, she realized it was the latter. Spider was working for his step father at his construction company.

Kyrah listened and laughed as he told her all about himself. Over the next two years, Spider spoiled her, picked up from school, took her everywhere she needed to go and snuck around with her to spend as much time as possible together. Her mother didn't approve of a twenty year old man dating her sixteen year old daughter and she had no problem letting him know it. She had even gone so far as to threaten him with jail time if he didn't stay away from her daughter.

Spider however had grown to love the spunky sixteen year old and Kyrah was far more advanced than her mother wanted to admit. Spider enjoyed her enthusiasm to be apart of his life in everyway, from going to work with him to her willingness to learn everything in bed to please him.

Hours upon hours she would listen to Spider talk about owning his own construction company someday. Kyrah had a brilliant mind and she knew that on the money he made working with his stepfather, his dream would never come true. She wanted him to be able to heavily provide for the family she planned to give him in the future.

When her mother passed away she used a protion of her mother's life insurance to give Spider the front money to get started in the game. She was down for whatever it took for her man to secure her future but as time passed on, Kyrah was beginning to dislike the man she saw unfolding in front of her eyes. Once they moved into the home they now shared on Emma and Spider really started hanging out in the hood all day everyday, he changed tremendously.

When he changed, Kyrah changed right along with him. No more were the days when he would come home to a hot meal, a clean home, his wife in sexy lingerie or anything of that magnitude. Kyrah had become bitter, bitter at all the empty promises and shattered dreams he had filled her head with.

Now they were more roommates than anything with the mutual responsibilities of taking care of the kids. Spider stayed away from home more and more now, mostly hanging out with his boys. He played around alot, yes but he never allowed any of them to interfere with home, not in such a way that the affair could totally destroy it; that was until now.

Spider took a hard swallow of his R&R chased by a swig of beer and laid his head back on the couch. He thought of how Mystic's lips felt to him earlier that day and for the time he didn't like it. He could tell her feelings towards him were changing. Her kiss felt forced and uninviting. He didn't want to lose her he told himself. She had come to mean so much to him.

If only she wasn't so close in the hood.

Spider wondered if there was a way he could make this work. He could work around doing business with Remo, that wasn't an issue for him. There may be a few ripples from the fallout but Spider didn't care.

Prez he had know for so long and they had done so much dirt together but Spider had to wonder could he ever really trust hin again. After the run in they had on Prez's porch over Mystic and Remo, Spider just didn't know anymore.

He took another gulp of the R&R and sighed a deep breath. The reason things were so haywire in his world was because he had allowed too many people in his business concerning Mystic and he could blame no one but hinself for taking her around niggah's he knew was scandelous.

Bad boys, real bad boys move in silence, he could hear his dad saying to him.

Spider realized that he had put Mystic in situations that she wasn't anywhere near equipped to handle. He expected her to know certain things like Kyrah who was seasoned in the game. He needed to understand that Mystic wasn't Kyrah and as he looked over at the TV and listened to Keisha Cole's Video, *Love* playing through the surround sound systeem, Spider accepted the fact that it was him and him alone who had set their relationship up to fail. He could no longer blame Mystic for the things that he should have not put her in a position to do.

"... love, never knew was I was missing but I knew once we started kissing, I found love....

The one thing Spider was certain of was that he didn't want to be without Mystic. He knew the pressure he had put on her to have an abortion was pushing her away from him and he'd never wanted to feel what he had felt in her kiss again. After all, he assured himself, a baby together would ensure she'd be in his life always in some form.

He reached over and picked up his cell phone from the seat cushion beside him, strolled down the contacts and rested on his cousin Shelby who had a lot of rental property on the southside of town.

As the phone rang in his ear he felt confident that he could make this work as long as they kept everyone out of their business.

"What's good cuz? I need a favor."

Shelby filled him in on what properties she had available and as she talked, Spider began to imagine a new life with Mystic along with their unborn child and for the first time in a long time… it excited him.

Chapter Fifteen

Mystic stood in the doorway to Cocamo's room, looking over at his bed. She couldn't believe she was standing there. She had the cozy blue towel wrapped around her, arms folded in front of her and a chill running down her spine from the soft breeze blowing through the open window.

Mystic was so nervous. She hadn't been with another man since she'd come home from prison besides Spider. She didn't count Remo because the situation wasn't a situation she enjoyed nor felt the need to perform. His touch had disgusted her in ways she couldn't have imagined but this was very different. Cocamo had a reputation in the streets among the ladies for being a beast in bed and Mystic wasn't sure if she'd be able to keep up.

Cocamo had set her body on fire with just the touch of his lips against hers. When he'd washed her body in the shower she felt an innocence she hadn't felt since she was a child. He was so gentle, so against the grain of what she had expected. She closed her eyes as she thought back to the way his voice sounded in her ear.

"I don't know what the fuck is gonna happen tomorrow. I can't stand here and tell you that I won't fuck with Tee-Tee again. What I can tell you is that despite all this shit, since the first muthafuckin' time I saw you step out that front door, next to me, I wanted this moment with you."

He pressed his body up against her ass as she leaned against the front door to leave. He ran his hands up her sides.

"I ain't trying to wife you; take you away from a muthafucka that don't deserve you or any of that shit. I just wanna feel the inside of you. Fuck you 'til the bottom fall out that pussy."

Mystic felt her heart rate increase and the muscles between her thighs tighten. She inhaled a deep breath and blew it out, slowly.

Can I really do this? I don't see why not? Everyone else around me is doing what the hell they wanna do, why shouldn't I? And look at who it's with. He's so fuckin' fine and I've thought of this moment several times myself, I can't lie.

Mystic felt the want in his voice and her body was screaming for her to indulge him. Like he said there would be no strings attached, just a night pleasure for the both of them.

Cocamo ran his hand up her chest and touched her lips with the tip of his finger. Mystic parted her lips and allowed her tongue to come out to greet his finger. Slowly he glided his finger in and out of her mouth.

That turned Mystic on beyond her wildest imagination. She didn't know if what was happening was right or wrong but at the moment she really didn't care. All that mattered was how he made feel inside.

Cocamo turned her to face him. He ran his hands underneath her sundress and up her thighs around to her ass. He gripped her cheeks so hard that he almost drew blood.

"I don't give a fuck how you feel about that niggah. I don't give a fuck that you carrying that niggah's seed. Look at me..."

Mystic tried to raise her eyes up to face him but she couldn't. Cocamo was so confident in his swag that it intimidated her.

She bit down on her bottom lip as he slid one of his hands around the front of her thigh to the middle of her essence. He slipped his finger under her panties and felt the juices meet his fingertip. He felt her clit began to jump and Cocamo slid his wet tip back and forth across it until Mystic felt weak in the knees.

"Look me in my eyes and tell me that letting me have you for one night is against the rules."

He lifted her right leg up around his waist and slid his fingers into the swamp she carried between her thighs.

Mystic raised her eyes to his as she panted with pleasure.

"I ...I ...can't...I can't..."

Cocamo curved his fingers and plunged deeper inside her. She glanced up at his face. He was so handsome to her. His skin so smooth, his lips traced by a finely shaped goatee and his dark eyebrows accented his pretty almond shaped eyes. Mystic could see the beam of the hallway light shining down on his dark wavy hair.

How could she deny herself of such a fine ass man? The sight alone of him was doing something wild to her.

"Is that a *no?*" he asked her leaning in to kiss her.

Mystic swallowed the lump in her throat and returned his kiss. She shook her head.

"No it's not."

"That's my girl. Don't cheat yo 'self, treat yo 'self. Give me yo' hand."

Mystic placed her hand inside his as he guided it down to the growing meat on the side his right leg. She closed her eyes as all doubts and thoughts of right or wrong went out the window.

"I know you want it. If you want it then tell me you want it."

He placed his hand on top of hers and squeezed it against his jimmy. Mystic felt it pulsate inside her palm and it sent a shock wave of electricity through her body.

Did she want him? She was dying to feel him.

"Yes," she whispered as he brought his tongue out to meet hers. Their tongues played together with so much friction it could've set them both on fire.

"Yes, yes I want it. I want you Coco."

Cocamo dropped her leg from around his waist, removed his fingers from inside her and kissed her on top of her nose. He told her he would be right back and to wait right there.

Mystic laid her head back against the door and touched her lips with her finger tips. She smiled at the thought of being with him. If ever she had an opportunity to change her mind it was then but Mystic wanted this night more than anything. The man she loved had so much as told her that he didn't want her to have his child and that no matter how much he loved her; he would never give up his family for her.

She felt un-needed, un-pretty and un-loved. A man like Cocamo wanting her, even if it was only for the night, made her feel wanted and she planned to engulf herself in the moment.

Cocamo returned to the hallway and waved for her to come to him. When she reached the bathroom door, he told her to undress and get into the shower he had started for her. He began to undress as well and Mystic turned away.

"What you looking away for? Come 'mere," he said, pulling her close to him. "Finish."

Mystic looked at him as she unbuttoned his belt and unsnapped his shorts. She looked down as his shorts hit the floor, exposing his jimmy poking out his boxers at a 90° angle. Her breathing told him she was excited as she put her fingers inside the rim of his boxers and pulled them down to the floor as well.

She bit the bottom of her lip thinking of how he would feel inside her. She hadn't been this turned on before, not even with Spider.

Cocamo lifted her sundress over her head and tossed it next to them on the floor. The steam from shower was creating a light sweat on her brow and it aroused him intensely.

He slid her panties to the floor, stood back and smiled at the site standing before him. Her breasts were round and perky. Her waist was small, sitting atop a pretty set of hips and thighs. Her ass wasn't too bad either.

Cocamo pulled back the curtain and guided her into the tub. He grabbed the soap and wash-cloth and gently began to bathe his tasty dish for the night.

Now Mystic stood in the doorway waiting for him to finish changing the sheets on his queen sized bed. He walked up to her, removed the bangs in her hair from her eye and told her to lie down on the bed.

"On second thought, forget the bed. I want something different with you," he said, passing her in the doorway and walking back towards the kitchen door. He had something better in mind for her.

"Come 'mere."

He took Mystic to the back yard, walked her over to a nearby ladder, and told her to wait. She watched as he climbed the ladder with a blanket, a small battery operated radio and pillow in hand. Mystic eyes lit up at the thought of making love to him on the roof.

Unc had a flat roof top and Cocamo had always wanted to knock one down up there, he just hadn't found the right one. Since he and Mystic had agreed that this would be the only night they would share, Cocamo decided to go all out. He thought it would be Tee-Tee but he didn't mind that he was wrong. Being with Mystic was like fulfilling a fantasy in his mind so thoughts of Tee-Tee weren't welcomed. This night, this night he would make sure that no matter what happened it would be one that Mystic would never forget it.

He came back down the ladder and told Mystic to climb up in front of him. When they reached the top, he laid her down onto the blanket and lay down beside her. He looked her in the eyes as he pulled apart the belt to his blue robe she was wearing and flung the flaps to the side, exposing her body to the moonlight.

He ran his hand across her breasts and took a hard swallow. She was beautiful to him. Cocamo leaned in and whispered in her ear.

"The shit I'm about to do you, ain't never been done before, not by me. First I gone erase all doubts and insecurities you got. No woman has ever been up here, you are the first. You know that I'm a private nigga and I don't let muthafucka's in my business so this won't go any further than here, not by me. I said that to say that, if this is the one chance, the one night we get, then I want to fulfill my fantasies with you and only you."

He towered above her.

"I'm a get what I want, I always do."

He placed his knees between her legs and slid them apart.

"You gone get what you want too."

He slid down, wet his lips and began to kiss her erect nipples one by one. His lips nestled snuggly around her breasts as he tugged on its built in pacifier. He bit down on each one aggressively.

Mystic wrapped her arms around his head. If felt so good to her. More so than the physical stimulation, was the mental pleasure that she would've never believed that in a million years that she would be there with him at that moment in time.

The radio was playing the love making music of R-Kelly's, *12 Play*.

"... *1... We'll go to my room for fun, 2... Then I'll say give me your tongue, 3... Cause tonight I'm gonna fulfill your fantasy yeah. 4... Lie down on the floor, 5... Cannot wait to cum inside, 6... Anything that's broken, I'll fix. ..."*

Cocamo guided his moist tongue down her stomach and off to the inside creases of her thighs. Her body damn near convulsed as he placed small bites on her most sensitive areas.

Mystic opened her eyes and was amazed at the sight they saw. The stars were blinking, the sky was dancing and the moon lit their way to ecstasy. Mystic took a deep breath and exhaled at its beauty as she felt Cocamo's finger touch her clit.

Her body tingled at his touch and Mystic gripped his shoulders. She couldn't believe he was so intimate and passionate. He caressed the throbbing mound of tissue with his lips until Mystics legs locked, her nails buckled down in his skin, her breath became short and her moans more intense.

For Cocamo to be such a rough neck, he took Mystic to higher heights as gently as cotton soaked in baby oil. She kept her eyes open as her body exploded. She felt as if Heaven was sending her a gift and she gladly accepted. She had thought that only Spider could have brought her to that level but the truth was, she had never experienced the feeling she was now feeling. The fact that Cocamo had done it without even being inside of her simply overwhelmed her. She was afraid; afraid at the possibilities he could do to her body once inside her.

Cocamo returned to her lips, told her to open her mouth.

"Taste yourself."

Mystic welcomed his tongue and its savory flavor as she slid her hand down to his jimmy.

"I want to taste you too." she whispered.

Cocamo put his finger to his lips.

"Shh... in due time, open up."

Mystic spread her legs on command and he entered her with an unsustainable passion. She was tight and he loved the way her walls felt around him. He worked his way inside and felt the heat of her walls welcome him.

"... 7... Spread your legs apart, 8... Feel me, I'm so hard, 9... See I want you from behind, with that bump and grind yeah, 10... Baby climb on top of me, 11... Up and down we'll go you'll see, 12... And that's when I go down on my knees giving you some of my twelve play..."

With a mixture of positions Cocamo brought Mystic a trio of orgasms that made her soul shake. He was gentle one minute and savage the next; ravishing her body like a raging wolf, then slowing like a woman caressing her new born baby.

Mystic loved every second they shared together. She creamed all over him in multiple fashions. On top, riding him like a stallion, on her back gazing up at the stars and on her knees giving him full access to the bottom of her tunnel.

The more he looked into her eyes and saw the expressions on her face, he couldn't bring himself to aloow her to be like the others. He wanted Mystic to stay respected in his eyes and remain special to him.

"You can't kiss me there, that ain't for you," he said, sliding his hands underneath her ass.

"I want you to stay pure to me, not like the rest. So consider this yo' night; It's all about you."

He slammed down inside her, pounding away at her flesh until he felt himself about to explode. For Cocamo the night wasn't about being the neighborhood big man or the hood's biggest player. That night was about sharing something special with a woman he wasn't sure he would ever get another chance to touch again.

When it was over, no words were spoken between them, none were needed. He kissed her softly on her forehead and Mystic fell into his touch once again. He stroked her hair as she rubbed her hand across his chest. Neither of them knew what tomorrow would bring and it didn't matter. If tonight was all they had, Cocamo had made it a night neither of them was sure to forget.

Mystic looked up at him when she heard him softly chuckling to himself.

"What's so funny?

"A nigga just got some pussy on the roof!"

Chapter Sixteen

Man eased up to the corner of Plover and Lillian Avenue, cut off his lights and shut down the jeep. He reached down underneath his seat and pulled out the shiny nickel plated .45. He checked to make sure it was fully loaded and patted his pocket for the extra ammunition he had stopped by the house to retrieve along the way.

Man had been on edge since his cousin had been killed. It's as if he was itching for a problem to come up he had to solve. Voilence wasn't a priority on his list but Man would go hard when necessary. After listening to Breeze earlier that day on top of what Prez had put Mystic through the night he had to go pick her up from the gas station, he felt that Prez was definitely a situation that called for a recipe for voilence; one cup of ass whipping blended with a half pound of .45 shells.

As he sat in his jeep waiting for the Champange colored Caddilac to return to it's home address, Man lit up a stoggie and blew the chronic smoke out the cracked driver's side window as he vibed off his favorite rapper's cd.

"...Got problems then handle it, these niggahs is jealous cause deep in they hearts they wanna be me. And now ya got me right beside ya, hopin' you listen, I catch you payin' attention to my ambition as a ridah..."

Things had just begun to be too much for Man to allow anything else to slide by or for anyone else to get a pass. His reputation in the hood was gained from the work he'd put in but Man had tried his best to settle down the gun play. Apparently Prez hadn't gotten the memo so every now and then Man had to deliver a lead telegram.

"... I won't deny it, I'm a straight ridah, you don't wanna fuck with me. I want money, hoes, sex and weed. I won't rest 'til my road dogs free..."

Man exhaled his smoke and smiled to himself as the caddi turned the corner to the left of him. Man watched closely as Prez crept by him and pulled over to the curb in front of his house. As he placed the roach in the ashtray, he leaned forward, placed his hand in the back of his waist and waited.

Prez had yet to exit the car so Man leaned back and thought of the two women he had now admittedly come to love in his life and their honors he felt compelled to protect. Breeze had become so much more to him than just a piece of pussy who grinded both for and with him. She had wiggled her way into into his heart and Man had gained a love for her he never thought a woman could make him feel. Mystic was a diamond to him and Man loved her in ways that some, even Breeze, may have felt was inappropriate but Man didn't care. He had never had any sexual thoughts of Mystic however; his love was protective and aggressive when it came to her. He wanted the best for the young skinny girl he had watched grow into a beautiful woman right before his eyes. Man felt that if she could only find a man who would assume the love he felt for her, he could and would reliquish some of the responsibility he felt toward her.

As it stood right now however, the job was his and it was a job he would proudly fufill as he watched his prey finally exit the car. Man slowly pulled back the door handle in the car and as quietly as he could, opened the door. Prez was talking on the phone and was distracted by both the caller and the MD 20/20 he'd been drinking all day.

Man hurried around to the side of the car three houses down from Prez but on the same side of the street. As Prez walked towards his front yard, Man silently crept up behind him. By the time Prez had the opportunity to react to the sound of the approaching footsteps, he felt the cold steel on the back of his neck and the click of the firing pin in his ear. Prez stiffened as his cell phone hit the ground and shattered at his feet.

Man stood behind him, leaned closely in his ear and with his best *Martin Lawrence* voice, he whispered, " When yo' lightened ass woke up this morning, I bet by eleven you didn't think yo' bitch ass was gone die, huh niggah?"

Prez's breathing got heavier, his voice choked inside his chest and he couldn't make a sound. That split second seemed to last a life time. Man ordered Prez to stand still as he searched around his waist for the gun Man knew he carried. He found it nestled in the front of his waistline. Prez had no idea who it was standing behind him nor that the women he crossed paths with would one day come back to bite him in the ass this way. Apparently he didn't know Man too well.

Man pressed the barrel of his .45 hard against Prez's back and told him to start moving.

"Over there between them two vacant houses niggah."

Prez saw his life start to flash before his eyes and he would do anything to not to lose it. He assumed the gunman wanted money and began offering up his cash in exchange for the opportunity to see another day.

"Aey homey, this ain't even gotta go down like this. What you need, money? I got money on me home boy; you can get it with no static from me. If that's not enough I got more in the crib. It ain't gotta be like this."

Man snickered.

"Niggah I don't want yo' money; I got my own fuckin' money! I'm so sure I got more than you. Now, what I do want is for yo' bitch ass to turn around and face me like a fuckin' man. I don't shoot niggah's in the back; that's for cowards. I like a niggah to look me in the eyes when I pull the trigger and put his ass to sleep. Now turn the fuck around!" Man commanded.

Prez slowly turned around and almost shit himself when he recognized the man holding the gun. Man was standing there with his pistol in one hand and Prez's in the other, both aimed at him.

"Never thought it huh niggah?"

"Come on dawg, what's this all about? I ain't got no beef with you, never have so what's good?"

Man cocked the pin on Prez's gun. They were now both locked and loaded.

"That's what you think and because I'm such a fuckin' gentlemen at this shit, I'm gone tell you why you was wrong in thinking that. You recall when yo' boy got popped and needed bond money? His bitch ass sent my gal's lil' sister to you to collect his chips. Next thing I know, I get a phone call, she cying and shit cause yo' ragedy dick ass put her out the car in O'Fallon Park in the dark. You recall that?"

Prez lifted his hand up in a surrendering motion. His eyes showed his fear and the wet spot expanding in between his thighs did as well.

Man smirked at the sight.

"So this is what bitch niggah's do when they about to die? And you trying to make muthafucka's suck that lil' uncontrollable shit?"

"Come on Man," Prez said, his voice quivering. "This ain't fo' us. We can let this ride and nobody will ever hear about from me. We good."

"It became for us when you set up my folks up to get robbed. Oh and it definitely became for us when yo' punk ass tried to disrespect me and shoot at my gal for some head over at yo' crib!"

Prez continued to plead with Man for his life but Man wasn't moved. He moved closer to Prez and asked him to give him one reason why he shouldn't blow his damn head off. Prez told him that he knew some information that he knew would be more valuable to Man than Breeze or Mystic could ever be.

Man stood back on his heels curiously and told Prez that he had sixty seconds to change his mind and let it flow.

"55, 54, 53…"

"I got something I know you wanna hear," Prez whimpered.

"49, 48, 47…"

"You lost somebody a while back right?"

"40 niggah, 39, 38, 37…"

"Yo' lil' cousin, right?"

Man walked up closer to Prez. If he didn't spit it out within the next few seconds, Man was going to say fuck the rest of the countdown and fill his ass full of holes.

"What the fuck you know about my lil' cousin? 19, 18…"

"Aight, aight… I know who shot him," Prez said as Man guestured with his gun for Prez to get down on his knees.

"Fuck this counting shit!"

Man pointed the gun at Prez's head and chest.

"That niggah Spider shot him! Spider killed yo' cousin homey. Spider said that yo' people set up Spider to get jacked by some niggah's over on the Horse Shoe and Spider caught up with him later that night and murked him. I swear to you man, that's on my kids."

Man stood paralyzed for a moment in disbelief.

It couldn't be, he told himself. *I know that niggah that fuckin' stupid!*

Man shook his head in disagreement.

"You lying niggah, I know you lyin'! You just tryin' to save yo' own ass!"

Man couldn't believe it. He thought back to the day his cousin had died. Spider wasn't acting differently when he saw him over at Mystic's house. Then Prez said something that forced Man to pay question that maybe he was telling him the truth.

"Ask yo' gal's sister where she hid the gun for that niggah. I ain't gotta lie! I'm tellin' you what I know! Ask her!"

Man's head began to spin over the thought that Mystic possibly knew anything about his cousin's death and didn't say anything to him. He couldn't even begin to wrap his mind around that but he would find out later, that's for sure. For right now, he had to focus on the task at hand.

"You lucky mutherfucka; you temporarily bought yo'self a pass," Man said, removing his finger from the trigger of his gun.

He had to get back to the block and find out what the fuck was going on. He refused to believe Mystic would ever cross their friendship like that. In the game casualties were to be expected but to Man, family was always off limits and if nothing else, he felt that Spider should have come to him and at least talked to him.

Man turned to walk away and head for his jeep as Prez stood up to dust off his clothes. Just as Prez smirked to himself, thinking he was in the clear, Man stopped dead in his tracks, turned around and sucked his teeth.

"You know what? On second thought…"

Man raised Prez's gun to him and began firing rounds into his chest and stomach. Prez tried to turn and run but Man dropped him with the first shot. He walked up to him and from close range continued to fire round after round until Prez's gun was out of ammunition. He had reached overkill.

As Man watched him take his last breath, he chuckled to himself.

"I know you didn't think you was really gone get a pass for that shit! Ole snitch ass niggah!"

Chapter Seventeen

Spider had left Mystic a message the last time he called and told her that he would be stopping by to talk to her. He was kind of excited about telling her about the apartment his cousin had gotten for them and the fact that he wanted her to keep the baby.

After the night Mystic had spent with Cocamo she didn't even know why she cared that he was coming by but she did. She'd listened to his voicemail over and over again and she could tell that it was something exciting in his voice. She really did want things to be different between them, she didn't know exactly how but she did. After the night before, her outlook had changed.

Cocamo showed her that someone other than Spider was capable of making her feel like the woman she'd always longed to be. Since she had gotten out of the halfway house and made it onto the block, Spider had been the only object of her desire.

She had wanted him so badly that she would do anything to be with him. She had done things against her nature not to mention the law just to be by his side. Now as she sat back on the bed, listening to the radio, she was beginning to realize that Spider probably wouldn't have done the same for her. All the sweet talk, all the game, all the lies and the bullshit… she had fallen for it all.

She felt like such a fool. She coud hear Cocamo's voice in her ear.

I ain't trying to wife you or take you from a muthafucka that don't deserve you…

His words had sent chills through her body.

Suddenly she heard a tap at her window. Mystic jumped from her thoughts and stood up on her bed to unlatch the window. She pulled it towards her and there stood Spider.

"Come open the door."

Mystic hurried up the steps and answered the door. When she saw him standing there, the look on his face was reminiscent of the night he showed up at her door with his shirt stained with blood all down the front. He had something on his mind and whatever it was, Mystic knew it was serious.

Spider entered the living room and stood in front of her. His mind was soaring in a million different directions and as he stood there staring in her eyes; all he could think about was what a little bird had told him a few hours earlier.

Tee-Tee couldn't wait for Spider to emerge from around the corner. She's sat up on RJ's porch across the street from Get Down's house and waited for Spider to hit the block.

What she had to tell him was burning a hole in her throat and when she finally seen him coming up Harney and pull over in front of Get Down's house, she leaped off the top step and headed across the street.

"What it do homie? I been here all evening waiting to holla at yo' ass," she told him, giving him some dap.

Her heart was bursting with raw emotions of anger and pain. She'd come around the block to holla at Cocamo after grinding on the set for most of the day. When she reached the top of the alley way of Mimika and Shulte she saw Cocamo entering his house followed by Mystic. She didn't really think too much of it because Mystic and Cocamo were neighbors and friends. She also knew that Mystic was totally wrapped up in Spider to even think about chasing after anyone else.

She had however tripped off the way Cocamo acted when they saw Mystic crying on the porch after Spider dropped her off the morning before. It was as if it was someone he loved a great deal that was in pain but she shook that off and assumed the visit was simply for them to discuss the reason she was so upset. Tee-Tee didn't want to intrude on their conversation and she knew how Cocamo hated when people dropped by unannounced so she decided to hang out on "Lil' Curtis' porch with his mom and brother down the way until Mystic left. In the meantime, she would call and let him know she'd be stopping by later.

He didn't answer her call; not none of the six times she dialed him and Tee-Tee grew more and more frustrated as a few minutes turned into an hour and that hour turned into several.

Once the sun had begun to set and Cocamo hadn't returned any of her calls, Tee-Tee's uneasy feelings began to get the best of her. She wanted to know what was going on inside that so important between the two of them that he couldn't answer nor return her calls. She walked off Lil' Curtis' porch and began walking up the block to get a closer look and what she found had built up so much emotion inside her that she was like a dam of information ready to burst. Once she started talking to Spider, she did just that.

Spider slapped her five and wrapped his arm around her. He always had so much respect for Tee-Tee and the way she moved in the game. He knew a lot of niggah's in the game that didn't have the nature or the heart of the hustle like Tee-Tee.

He asked her what she needed to speak to him about.

"Man, it's a lot of foul shit been going on over across that street in the last 24," she told him, nodding towards Mystic's house. "I mean, me and Coco was outside the morning you dropped her off right and I been sensing something's been up between them cause that niggah ain't usually that worried about nobody but his damn self.

Lil' Momma came home crying and he damn near broke his neck to see what was wrong with her. So you know I ain't too much trip off it at that moment. Then last night I was coming through to holla at Coco, I see him and ole' girl going in the crib, his crib. So I decided to chill and wait for a minute cause I'm knowing they cool like that. No big deal, right? I'm blowing this nigga phone off the hook but he ain't answering. So finally, I'm talking *hours* done passed niggah and I finally decide to go up to the crib and see what the fuck is going on."

Spider's eyebrows raised in curiousity. He was praying she wasn't about to deliver no more news about Mystic to him that was going to piss him off. He was so siked about sharing his news with her.

"He got the blinds and shit shut," Tee-Tee continued. "So I goes around to his window on the side of the house to see if they in the bed room. They closed too, so I get ready to walk around to the back and as soon as I stepped around, I see him and Mystic coming out the back door. So I'm like *what the fuck?*"

Spider bit down on the inside of his jaw as he waited for the punch line to the story.

"So?" he asked her, lighting up a cigarette.

"So he took this bitch up on the roof! She came out wearing his bathrobe and all that niggah had on was a pair of shorts and shit. He had a pillow in his hand and a blanket. So unless I'm a dumb bitch, they was on the way up on the roof to be on some real freaky shit. And you know I'm a night owl so I came over here to RJ's crib so I could see how long she was gone be there. Well, let's just say Shirley Murdoch said it best niggah when she said, *its' morning and we slept the night away,"* she sang animated.

Spider looked off across the street and back to Tee-Tee. He blew out the smoke from his Newport and sighed. How much more was he going to have to take when it came to Mystic; it seemed like everytime he turned around, there was someone telling him something about a niggah being between her legs. He was boiling on the inside.

"So you trying to tell me that she fuckin' that niggah Cocamo too? Please tell me that that is not what you saying Tee?"

"Niggah I ain't *trying* to say shit, I'm telling you what the fuck I know!"

Spider told Tee-Tee he had some business to take care of but that he would holler back at her later. He was trying to surprise Mystic with the key to their love nest but now, he just needed to go somewhere and cool off. He jumped in his truck and sped off. He stopped by the F&G, grabbed him two pints of R&R and headed down West Florissant to O'Fallon Park.

As he sat back in the truck, listening to the radio, he allowed the R&R to fuel his rage.

"*...all this time I been sleeping with you, you been sleeping with me; you been stroking him and loving him and kissing him and hugging him. And while you been creepin' with him, he's been sexing yo' friends; now I got you thinin' about it, thinkin' about it....why must I endure, your constant greed, your endless need to* *be so damn freaky? Now I understand, that it wasn't me... yes payback's a mutha baby...."*

Spider didn't know what to do with the emotions he felt. He was out of control and this time he aimed to take them out on the one person he felt was the cause and cure. He had finally decided to let the shit go with Remo and now Cocamo? The deal with Remo he had decided was forgivable because she had done a dumb thing but with his best interest at heart. This shit with Cocamo she done because she wanted too, plain and simple. Now here he stood in front of her, his anger flaring up inside of him.

"You wanna go downstairs and talk?" she asked him.

"Naw, we good right here. I need to ask you a question and spare me the bullshit when you answer. You fucked that niggah next door?"

His question had caught Mystic off guard.

How in the hell?

"Yeah, that niggah told me," he lied, approaching her.

He wouldn't... why would he do that to me?

Mystic couldn't believe her ears. She'd thought that he was different from the rest of the niggah's on the block but then again, her judge of character when it came to the men in her life hadn't been the best. Still she had thought that the night they had shared was special. Apparently she was wrong.

She didn't know what to say to Spider. No matter the answer, she knew it would hurt him and make things that much worse between the two of them.

"Spi... Spider... I'm... I'm really sorry. I thought that we, you and I... I thought that we were over. It was that one time and..."

Slap!

To hear her say it aloud snapped something inside of him and before he knew it, his open hand made contact with her face, hard.

Mystic grabbed her cheek in horror. She couldn't believe he had just raised his hand to her. She was afraid, very afraid.

"What the fuck is wrong with you? You just slutting yo'self out all over the place! You fucking er'thang walking ain't you? And don't give me that bullshit about trying to help me cause that shit don't fly this time!"

Mystic backed herself up against the wall, still in shock over what had happened.

"I can't believe you hit me," she whispered.

"Well believe it! You running around here fuckin' muthafucka's right and left and claiming you carrying my seed? *My* muthafuckin' seed? I got put out my house, went though all this retarded shit and yo' nasty ass is fuckin' doing it like that?"

Spider could no longer control the anger inside him. The two pints of R&R didn't help none. He grabbed Mystic by her throat and slammed her back into the wall. Her head hitting the white dry wall hard enough to leave a crack. She felt a sharp pain shoot down her back and thought she was going to pass out. His grip was so tight that she became light headed. She tried her best to pry his hand from around her neck.

"I...I...can't...breath," she whimpered through her tears.

Spider had enough rage in him to snap her throat in two but he let her go and threw her down onto the grey carpet below. On and on he ranted as Mystic grabbed her throat and gasped for air. There was no where to run and no one to call for help in the house. Punkin was gone out with her friends and Mystic hadn't heard Breeze come in either. She thought she was alone but the thump of her hitting the floor so hard had awakened a sleeping Breeze whose room was right below the living room.

When Breeze sat up in her bed and focused in on the noises she heard above her, she jumped up and ran upstairs to her sister's aide. When she reached the living room and saw Mystic on the floor grabbing her throat and trying to breath, she ran over and hovered above her little sister.

"What the fuck is wrong with you niggah? Who the fuck do you think you are? You better get the fuck outta here before I stab yo' ass!" Breeze said, point at the door.

"This ain't yo' business Breeze!"

"Niggah this *my* lil' sister, fuck you mean? She is my business and I ain't gone tell yo' ass again! Get out of here!"

Spider reached down around Breeze and grabbed Mystic's wrist as Breeze got up and ran into the kitchen and grabbed a butcher's knife and the phone. She made two phone calls. One to Man and the other to Unc. Unc wasn't in so she'd told Cocamo what was happening, not know that he was the reason that they were into it.

When Breeze returned to the living room she snatched Mystic away from Spider's grasp.

"Niggah we ain't never had no beef but if you put yo' muthafuckin' hands on my sister one more time, I'll kill yo ass, I swear I will!"

Breeze told Spider that she had called the police and that he had five seconds to get the hell out of their house before they arrived.

Spider stood huffing and puffing, staring at both of them as if he wanted to hurt them both.

"And to think I went and got an apartment for yo' ass! I was coming here to tell you that I wanted to move you away from here so you could keep the baby and I could be there with you. And this the shit I gotta deal with? You ain't shit! You just like the rest of these scheming bitches! I tried to make you into somethin' but you know what you are?"

"Get the fuck out Spider!" Breeze yelled. "I'm not gone say it again!"

Spider finally walked to the door and looked back at her. She could see the hurt in his face.

"Trick!" he spat out on his way out the door.

On his way down the steps, he passed Cocamo coming across the driveway. Spider didn't break stride, he just continued on to his truck.

"What's up niggah?" Cocamo asked him, his hand in the back of his waist nestled around his gun.

"Shit ain't nothin', she all yours homie."
Spider jumped in his truck and sped off up the block.

"I didn't think so, bitch ass niggah!"

Cocamo waved him off and headed up the steps, into the house. He didn't see anyone in the living room, the kitchen or the bathroom. He yelled down the steps and Breeze told him to come on down. She was placing a towel filled with ice on Mystic's cheek and lip which had a pretty bad cut on it from Spider's ring.

When Cocamo entered the room, he walked over to the bed and looked down at her. Instantly he was enraged on the inside. He didn't hit women and couldn't stand a niggah that hit women either. To him that was the cowards move.

Breeze stood up so Cocamo could sit down on the bed beside Mystic. Man was coming down the steps so Breeze stepped out into the hallway to greet him.

With a moment alone, Mystic took the time to ask Cocamo why he had betrayed her.

"Why did you tell him? Why would you do that?" she uttered as she reached up and grabbed his shirt, pulling him towards her. "He said he did this because you told him we spent the night together."

Mystic began to cry.

Man and Breeze were standing in the doorway at the time, neither of them aware that Mystic and Cocamo was kicking it with one another. They stood by in shock as Cocamo explained to her that Spider had lied to her.

"You should know me better than that but apparently you don't. I don't move like these bitch made niggah's around here baby. So I ain't told that niggah shit! I don't get down like that; me and that niggah ain't that fickin' close. We ain't homies, we ain't partner's and we ain't muthafuckin' friends, so how do I look telling that niggah my damn business. Use yo' brain and think! He's a bitch! And I don't do bitches! Not the ones with dick's between they legs anyway!"

He wiped her face with the palm of his hand.

"But I will tell you this," he continued. "I'm finna fuck him up!"

"*We* finna fuck him up!" Man chimed in from the doorway.

He was already planning Spider's demise and seeing Mystic laying there bruised up had just sealed his fate.

Man locked eyes with Cocamo and they both headed out the door. Mystic lay there, tears rolling down her cheeks and wondered how Spider could ever raise his hand to her.

She felt so stupid for loving him the way she did. She'd ignored all the warnings from those closest to her and had allowed herself to become entangled in all his madness. How many times had eveyone told her that she wasn't ready for this side of the game?

Breeze peeked her head back inside the door.

"You know they meant what they said right? His ass is grass."

Mystic lay back on the pillow and as the hurt gave way to anger, she decided that this wasn't Man and Cocamo's responsibility fight; it was hers. She was the one who had caused so much of this and it was her mess to clean up.

How the fuck he gone act like I'm the one who did wrong? He's the niggah that's married, he went to jail and I'm the only one who gave a fuck about him coming home! And you hit me?

Mystic got up out the bed, walked out the room, peeked into Breeze's room and found her back in bed. Mystic quietly walked over to the wash room, quietly removed the top from the drain and reached down inside. She grabbed the steel wrapped in plastic and removed it from down inside the drain. She stood up, hid the bag underneath her shirt and tip-toed back to her room.

She sat down on the bed and as quietly as she could, unwrapped the bag and pulled the contents from inside. She grabbed the old shirt it was wrapped in and opened it. She stared down at the gun and contemplated what to do. She felt the tear roll down her face as she looked at herself in the mirror on her dresser. Her face was really starting to swell.

She wasn't sure if it was anger or hurt that made her pick up the phone and dial 911 but she did.

Mystic stared off at the wall and the Asian operator asked her for the third time, "Ma'am, what's your emergency?"

Mystic looked at her stomach, her face and back to her stomach.

"Hello is anyone there?" the operator asked again.

"Yes… yes I'm here… can you transfer me to someone?"

Mystic paused.

"I…I got..."

"Ma'am what is it?"

"I got information on a murder."

Chapter Nineteen

Cocamo pulled the grey '84 Pontiac he borrowed from one of his customers up to the top of the alley at Era, cut off the lights and handed Man the blunt he was smoking.

Man inhaled as he thought back to what Prez had told him about Mystic.

"No way she knew what the situation was when she hid that gun fo' that niggah," Man said.

"You know just as much as I do that Mystic would never do you like that. She too crazy about you. You like a brother to that girl. You couldn't pay me to believe otherwise," Cocamo assured him.

"Yeah I feel you," Man told him, handing him back the blunt. "But umm, when did you and lil' momma start kickin' it? I was in the door way like *what the fuck*; when did this shit shit start?"

Cocamo chuckled.

"It just kinda went there. Neither one of us planned it. You know we both had other shit goin' on so it wasn't like we was trying to get at each other. The shit just flowed niggah."

"So what about ole girl?"

"That ain't even an issue fo' me no more. I cancelled that check. I'm just feeling Mystic man and it ain't just start, I just decided to stop fightin' it, feel me?"

"It's all good, she need that," Man said, giving him some dap with his fist. "But niggah let me tell you about this lame ass niggah Prez. You should've seen that niggah face when he recognized who I was. This niggah started testifying like he was at Sunday confession."

They both laughed.

"Niggah pissed on himself when he heard the pin cock. And this niggah, I can't wait to dig up in him. I ain't never had no beef with him but this shit don't get no pass from me. I done seen this niggah everyday since my lil' cousin got murked and he know the shit I been on. He had to know I would eventually find out. He had ample opportunity to holla at me. I even sat out in the school yard with this niggah when I told him about the ill shit Prez did with his gal."

Cocamo looked at him strangely. Man knew Mystic hadn't told him.

"When this niggah went to jail and needed some money to make bond, he sent Mystic to meet up with ole' boy cause apparently he had some dough he owed Spider. Long story short, the bitch ass niggah takes her in the park and asks her for some dome. When she says no, he put her out in the park."

Cocamo damn near choked on his weed.

"Yeah, now that there is a recipe that calls for some lead seasoning, you hear me. These lame ass niggah's out here be straight trippin'," he said, handing the blunt to Man.

He was getting more irritated with Man's every word. He smiled inside as he thought back to her laying on the couch across from him earlier that evening, looking over at him.

"Why you looking at me like that? What's on yo' mind? This is a no-holds-barred crib over here. By all means, you got something on yo' mind, let it off."

Mystic bit down on the bottom of her lip and looked out the front window.

"Why me Coco?" she asked softly. "I mean you're Coco... you're..."

"Why me?" he interupted. "You're Mystic."

That made her smile which in turn made him smile.

Man hit him on the chest to hand him back the blunt, bringing Cocamo back to the scene with him.

"You know me Coke, you know that if a muthafucka come tell me that my lil' cousin was on some ill shit I would've handled it and kicked him back down his grip. That's how I get down. This niggah *had* to know I would come fo' that ass, he had to."

Cocamo laid his head back onto the head rest and reflected on Mystic's words in his ear.

He said you told him.

He was so perplexed as to how the niggah could have found out Mystic was over to his house. Tee-Tee had blown his phone up all evening.

Maybe she saw Mystic come inside.

That or either Spider was stalking her. He didn't give a fuck how he found out for real because Cocamo knew that Spider would never come at him cross. He knew Cocamo long enough to know that he would drop him where he stood.

The look on Mystic's face when he entered her bedroom had enraged him. The swelling told him that Spider had struck her with heavy force. Cocamo would be sure to return the favor to him.

He had let Mystic go home against his better judgement that evening. They had spent the evening having dinner watching *The Wood* and just trying to keep their minds on things that were pleasant and giving themselves a break from the drama of the hood.

Cocamo felt that he could relax with Mystic knowing that her company and her interest in him was pure with no strings attached. It was actually him that was chasing her and that was a first for him so he knew that giving their friendship a chance to grow into something special was the right choice for him.

The love they made was untarnished and stemmed from an attraction of his heart, not his jimmy and Cocamo really enjoyed the way that felt.

Man jumped up in his seat as he spotted Spider exiting his front door. Cocamo cracked his window and tossed the blunt roach outside. He grabbed his gun from down underneath the front seat and hurried out of the car to catch up to Man who was already on his way across the street.

Cocamo ducked down behind the car and followed Man's trail across the street behind the van sitting in Spider's neighboring driveway. They watched as Spider stood smoking a cigarette at the edge of his front lawn and talking on his cell phone.

Cocamo nodded to Man as they headed across the grass and stopped within 15 feet of Spider's front yard.

Standing there, guns drawn and aimed his way, Spider dropped both the cigarette and the phone.

"What's this all about?" Spider asked, fearing for his life.

"You gotta ask?" Cocamo replied.

Man didn't have time for no more small talk. He had given Prez too much time to talk earlier and while it turned out to work in his favor, he was sick of bitch made niggah's trying to talk their way out of the enevitable. He wasn't in the mood for no more conversation.

He looked at the pistol in his hand and snickered to himself.

Take this with you curtesy of yo' pot'na.

Man squeezed the trigger and fired. Cocamo followed suit and together they sent a slew of bullets ripping through the air. You could hear the metal bouncing off Spider's truck and hear him screaming out in agony.

Man fired rounds for his cousin. Cocamo fired round for Mystic and in sync they fired for the game.

When Spider fell to the ground Man turned to head back down the alley but Cocamo walked closer to Spider. Man called out to him.

"What the fuck you doin'?"

Cocamo towered above Spider. He lifted the black ski mask from his face to allow Spider to see his identity.

"You never deserved her niggah. You couldn't give her shit cause you ain't shit. You think you tough cause you can put yo' hands on a woman? You ain't looking too tough now."

Man was yelling for Cocamo to hurry up.

Spider began to cough, blood seeping out of his mouth. He was hit in the left shoulder, his right arm, his left leg and his stomach. Wounds he probably could've recovered from but with Cocamo within inches from his face, Spider's life hung drastically in the balance.

"Get me…me… some help man, pl…please."
Cocamo stood up and shook his head.

"I got some help fo' that ass," he said as he fired a fatal shot into the center of Spider's brain.

Him and Man ran back into the alley, jumped into the car and sped off down Era towards West Florissant. They headed over to the west side to return the car to its owner and waited a few hours before returning to the hood. Each of them knew that the other would take this secret to the grave with them and neither of them regretted that it had to be done.

When he opened the door to Mystic's room, she was sitting up on her bed, watching the news. The gun she'd retrieved from the drain wrapped in a towel on the bed beside her.

Tears were streaming down her face.

Police identified the victim as 32 year old Marcus Johnson of the 5900 block of Emma. Police say the vitcim was standing in his front lawn when he was killed. Onto other news, police also found the body of 30 year old Preziver Copeland lying in an alleyway between two vacant houses on Plover earlier this evening. Police have no suspects at this time…

Cocamo walked into the room, put the towel containing the gun on the dresser, sat down beside her and wrapped his arm around her. He took the remote from her hand and cut off the TV.

He wiped her tears with his hand as he placed soft kisses on her forehead and cheeks.

"Come on, let me tuck you in," he told her.

Mystic stood up as Cocamo pulled back the burgandy satin covers on her bed and helped her down onto the bed. He grabbed her some tissue from the tiny blue box on her nightstand and handed it to her.

"I'll check on you in the morning; try to get some rest" he said, bending down to kiss her one last time.

Mystic watched him as he headed for the door. She didn't want him to go.

"Coco?"

"Yeah?"

"Will you stay with me?"

Cocamo didn't hesistant. He walked back over to the bed, slid off his shoes and climbed underneath the covers behind her. She scooted her body close to his and he held her tightly in his arms.

"You can rest now. I got you and I ain't never, never let a muthafucka hurt you again."

Man stood in the doorway, listening. He reached inside the room and flicked off the light switch on the wall. As he closed the door he finally knew in his heart that Mystic would be okay. She'd finally gotten what she always wanted; what she longed for and most of all, what she needed in her life... a real niggah.

Federal Prison Camp
- Only the Strong Survives

Prelude…

Inmate #89196-022

Charlene looked down at the Reciving & Discharge callout sheet and skimmed through it for her name. She smiled as she found it next to her appointment time of 0700 hours. Finally, she would be going home. For Charlene it had been a long, grueling four years and six months and now she was ready to move on with her life.

There would be some of the 342 women she would be leaving behind that she would miss tremendously. Those women that had been a surrogate family to her during the duration of her sentence from the county jail, to behind the gate to the camp she was now leaving in the morning. Faces she would never forget and keep in her memory forever.

These friendships were forged under the harsh circumstances of prison life but they were the realest she had ever been apart of. In prison she was at her lowest and so were the women around her and so she knew that their bonds were genuine. Unlike the street life where everyone tried to out shine everyone else; in prison they all wore the same blue prison issued suit, the same brand of tennis shoes, the same cheap deodorant and body oil. There was need to pretend; everyone knew what the other was feeling and that helped Charlene make it through some of her most difficult days on the inside.

"So you finally leaving huh?" he asked her, smiling as he stood over her shoulder looking down at the paper.

Charlene felt the heat of his breath on her neck and it nauseated her. He would be the one person she would be so glad that she would never have to see again.

Officer Tucker was a 280 pound, white man with skin like a sunburned lizzard. His face was full of pits and crates with pores that looked like potholes. His hair was greasy and you could smell his cheap cologne coming around the corner ten minutes before he did. His armpits always reeked and his look always put Charlene in the mind of pure trailer trash.

A Kentucky good ole boy, Officer Tucker was one of Warden Hanyes' favorite officers because he always went above and beyond his call of duty to keep the prison grounds safe. He was a stickler for the rules, except the ones he himself wanted to break. He was an officer the inmates in both the camp and the adjoining men's prison hated to see coming on the day of rotation because they knew they were constant shakedowns (when an officer goes through every little thing inside a prisoners cell looking for contraband; things the inmates weren't allowed to have), no bending of the rules and just an all around asshole on duty.

Each officer rotated for a three month term and most officers preferred the women's camp over the niose, violence and restrictions of the men's facility. The female camp held close to 350 women on any given day and only staffed one guard, one kitchen supervisor and one recreation specialist, two counselors and a camp administrator. With the eception of the second shift guard, all staff was gone no later than six pm. That left one man if on rotation alone to manage three hundres plus women at one time.

The camp was an open camp, meaning there were no bars, no gates and no locked doors to hold the females inside. The inmates were trusted to remain on the compound or pay the consequnces of an exscape charge which carried a mandatory five years added on to their present sentence and confinement back behind the gates. The camp brought primarily easy shift for the officers but Officer Tucker liked the rotation at the camp for another reason... power.

He was one of those men who out on the streets probably couldn't get laid unless he paid for it but on the inside he knew that there were desperate women, some who had been down (locked up) for as long as twenty years. There were those who had habits out on the streets and would do anything for a fix on the inside. There were also those who played the game of prison life, using their bodies to get what they wanted from the gaurds. Those he toyed with from time to time but the quests that gave him the most pleasure were the ones he had the joy of breaking down until they complied with his demands. Fantasy girls like Charlene he couldn't even wave to out on the streets.

Charlene was a twenty seven year old mother of two who came to prison after being convicted of drug trafficking for attempting to carry Cocaine on a plane from Ohio to Atlanta, which made it a federal offense.

Charlene was born and raised in Columbus, OH and for the most part stayed out of trouble. That all seemed to change when she met her children's father Marco when she was seventeen.

Marco was a dope dealer and Charlene got hooked on the lifestyle he dabbled in very quickly. The money he spent on her and gave to her, made her feel as if she was on top of the world. The shopping sprees, the designer handbags and shoes, the diamonds on her neck, ears and fingers.

She wasn't sure if she loved Marco the man or Marco the money but she dug her nails into him and gave him two children to seal her life with him. She understood that the game came along with many obstacles but she'd never imagined herself doing fed time, especially while her children's father was free out on the streets.

When Marco had asked her to make the drop for him, Charlene didn't hesistant because it wasn't the first, the second or the tenth time she'd done it for him. What she didn't know was that the connect receiving the dope had already been caught up on another case and was now co-operating with the Feds to pull people in.

When Charlene checked into the Delta Airline gate she was a little nervous as always but she knew that she had packed the drugs securely around her thighs with tape. She was instructed to place her carry on bag onto the roller and asked if she had anything liquid over the allowed weight of three ounces. Her bag cleared security and Charlene felt a little better. She took off her shoes, her bracelets and earrings and placed them into the grey container along with her cell phone.

When she walked through the metal detector, the underwire in her bra made the alarms go off. The awaiting Feds took the opportunity to have her stand off to the side for a personal search. Charlene was instructed to step inside a screening room where a female customs agent told her to remove all articles of clothing.

Charlene was wearing a very loose fitting sundress and when instructed to disrobe, she hesistantly slid the straps from her shoulders one by one and let them fall down to her side. The customs agent could sense something was wrong because of the way Charlene was acting.

The hefty Chinese woman walked closer to her and told her that she needed to speed it up. Charlene sighed and obeyed, letting the sundress fall to the floor. The custom's agent shook her head when she saw the powdered packages sealed in Suran wrap taped securely around each thigh.

Charlene was devestated. She had never been in any real trouble with the law and sitting in the Custom's office of the Port Columbus Airport, she had no idea what to do. She sat by helplessly as three DEA agents wheighed in the product, questioned her for over three hours about where she was going, who she worked for and telling her how she could help herself if she would just co-operate.

Charlene refused to answer any of their questions, even after the threats of a fifteen year sentence behind bars. She simply couldn't imagine turning on the father of her children. Charlene knew the risks when she decided to make the trip and so no, she would bare her own cross. Charlene stood her ground.

When she finally reached the Columbus Detention Center and was allowed to make a call, she called Marco. He already figured that she had gotten pinched because she hadn't called him and told him that she had made it through security.

"You good baby?"

"Yeah, I'm good. They was coming at me pretty hard though but shit, I stood on mines."

"Don't you worry about nothing, you hear me?" he said to her.

Charlene knew that Marco would hire the best attorney for her and he did. She pissed off the prosecution at every turn by refusing to help them in any fashion and they made it known to the judge at her sentencing hearing after she pled guilty to "possession with the intent to distribute."

When the judge handed down her six year sentence Charlene was pretty relieved. Yes it would hurt her to be away from her children and their father but the sentence could have been stiffer, a lot stiffer.

Marco had promised to hold her down while she was down and bring their children to see her every weekend. Charlene felt that with that promise, she would be okay and for the most part she was until about nine months ago when Officer Tucker took his much anticipated shift at the camp.

"Be downstairs by the computer lab right after count. I might as well get one off for the road," he said, polking her with his pelvis before walking off.

Charlene hated him and everything he stood for. Everyone knew it was against the law for an officer to sleep with an inmate and some officers refused to risk their jobs on what society deemed the scum of the earth. Officer Tucker however had a fettish and he used his power over the girls to feed it.

He wasn't concerned about getting reported because he could make their lives hell on the inside and that was the last thing Charlene wanted. Her visits and phone calls were all she had and she would lose her mind if they were ever taken away.

As he walked down the hallway and up the back stairs to her room, Charlene decided that her last day on the compound would be one that no one would forget. She had no choice but to meet him by the computer lab but this time she wouldn't be the only one who ended up regretting it.

Other Novels by Allysha Hamber

Unlovable Bitch, A Hoe is born

Unlovable Bitch II

Keep It On The Down Low, Nobody Has To Know

What's Done in the Dark, Will eventually Come To Light

The North Side Clit

Vashon High, Playing Hardball

Mimika Avenue, You Must Respect the Game

Coming Soon:

Federal Prison Camp, Only the Strong Survives

Contact the Author at:

Lele4you@Hotmail.com

www.facebook.com/allyshahamber

www.myspace.com/diamondclit

allysha4you@yahoo.com

Made in the USA
Charleston, SC
24 August 2013